50
True Tales
From Our Great
NATIONAL PARKS

50
True Tales
From Our Great
NATIONAL
PARKS

Written by Stephanie Pearson

Illustrated by Madeline Kloepper

WIDE EYED EDITIONS

Contents

Welcome to
the wild and wonderful world of America's National Parks . . .

The National Parks of the United States are a treasure trove of wild riches. They shelter a host of remarkable animals and precious plants and guard ancient histories of the land's original residents whose ancestors were here long ago. These parks are places of beauty and wonder with towering peaks, rushing rivers, and shifting sands. And they are also the settings of countless courageous human achievements.

Visiting one of these protected parks is an adventure like no other. You can see incredible natural wonders, like Old Faithful, a geyser spewing water 200 feet into the air at Yellowstone National Park! You can spot a thousand-pound leatherback turtle while swimming underwater at Dry Tortugas National Park. Or you can feel your triumphant heartbeat after reaching the top of Old Rag, a mountain in Shenandoah National Park.

No matter which park, there is so much to experience. Some day you may have the chance to visit all of them. Until then, let this book take you on a tour of these spectacular places through fifty true tales.

Each story takes place in a particular national park. Some tell tales of human bravery, exploration, and endurance, highlighting heroic men and women—like Polly Mead, the first female ranger in Grand Canyon National Park. Others describe fascinating plants and creatures, like the acrobatic humpback whales that dance in Glacier Bay National Park. Some delve into the past, exploring how certain parks were shaped by natural forces or retelling Indigenous histories, like the story of Pele, the goddess at the heart of Hawai'i Volcanoes National Park.

Today, the parks are places of protection and a welcoming oasis for all. But the creation of the parks was complicated, which is important to remember. So this book also contains some stories that explore the effects on Indigenous peoples and other communities that were driven off their lands to make way for the parks. After all, remembering the past, helps us to shape a better future.

Now, settle down, breathe in, and turn the page. It's time to step into the wonder of our great national parks and get lost in these tales. May each story inspire you to learn more, plan a visit, and help protect these beautiful places.

The U.S. is home to **sixty-three national parks.** This book explores tales from fifty of them, but **turn to pages 126-127** for a sneak peek at the other thirteen parks.

The National Parks of the USA

North Cascades

Glacier

Olympic

WA

MT

ND

Theodore Roosevelt

Mount Rainier

OR

ID

Yellowstone

SD

Crater lake

Grand Teton

Wind cave

Badlands

WY

Redwood

NE

Lassen Volcanic

NV

Rocky Mountain

UT

Arches

CO

Great Basin

Capitol Reef

Black Canyon of the Gunnison

KS

CA

Yosemite

Canyonlands

Bryce Canyon

Great sand Dunes

Pinnacles

Kings Canyon

Zion

Mesa Verde

Death Valley

Grand Canyon

NM

Sequoia

Petrified Forest

Channel Islands

AZ

White Sands

Joshua Tree

Carlsbad Caverns

Saguaro

Guadalupe Mountains

TX

Big Bend

Kobuk Valley

Gates of the Arctic

AK

Denali

Wrangell- ST. Elias

Haleakala

Lake Clark

Katmai

Kenai Fjords

Glacier Bay

Hawai'i Volcanoes

HI

Voyageurs

MN

Isle Royale

WI

IA

MI

IL

IN

Gateway Arch

MO

OH

KY

Mammoth Cave

AR

TN

OK

Hot Spring

MS

AL

GA

LA

FL

Indiana Dunes

Cuyahoga Valley

New River Gorge

WA

Shenandoah

Great Smoky Mountains

NC

Congaree

SC

Biscayne

Everglades

Dry Tortugas

NH

VT

ME

Acadia

NY

PA

VA

MA

RI

CT

NJ

DE

MD

D.C.

American Samoa

AS

US Virgin Islands

USVI

The Amazing Acrobats of Glacier Bay

Glacier Bay National Park and Preserve, Alaska

More than 250 years ago a giant glacier slowly advanced 100 miles across the mountainous slopes of southeast Alaska. The sheet of ice was a menacing beast, trampling trees and plants and chasing away wolves, brown bears, and even the Huna Tlingit people who had lived here for centuries. The glacier enveloped everything in its path and turned the deep green forest into a world of icy whiteness.

This freezing period known as the "Little Ice Age" didn't last forever. After few decades, the glacier began to melt away, slowly retreating up the valley from where it came.

Where the glacier once lay, something miraculous started to happen. The indentation left by the ice turned into a beautiful turquoise bay . . .

Today, there are more than 1,000 smaller glaciers, fragments from the Little Ice Age, left in what we now call Glacier Bay National Park. As they melt, big chunks of ice—some of them the size of a house—crash into the bay with a fierce and powerful force. Over the last century, spruce and hemlock forests have grown back, providing a home for brown bears, moose, and many other animals. In the sparkling blue waters, sea otters, sea lions, and orcas come out to play.

One creature in particular has found stardom here. The humpback whale is the largest marine mammal in the park. In spring, summer, and fall, these whales twirl and splash in the bay. They're here to feast on fish like herring and capelin. But that's not all, the whales also put on a show—an incredible whale ballet with practiced moves. First they leap, launching their giant bodies high in the air like rockets. Then they slap the water with their massive flippers, before splashing backward into the ocean.

Scientists believe this amazing acrobatic performance is more than just a dance. It's likely a way for these whales to communicate with each other because the splashing and slapping can be heard from miles away under the water.

In the late fall, most Glacier Bay humpbacks start swimming all the way to Hawai'i, where they mate and give birth in warmer waters. The 2,500-mile swim takes about a month each way. While the whales are traveling, they eat nothing. When their calves are finally born, between December and February, the babies weigh 2,000 pounds, about the size of an average car. As spring nears, the whales and their calves begin their long journey back to their home in Glacier Bay, where they can once again feast on fish and plankton and grace the waters of this park with their majestic dance.

Return to Paradise

Virgin Islands National Park, U.S. Virgin Islands

With its sparkling white sand beaches, crystal-clear waters, and thriving coral reefs, the island of St. John is a true Caribbean paradise. Back in 1956, almost two-thirds of this mountainous island became a national park. It is a place open to all, where visitors can view ancient rock carvings called petroglyphs made by the Indigenous Taino people; hike forested trails; or snorkel among colorful reef fish just a short swim offshore.

But one day, on September 6, 2017, a fierce storm named Hurricane Irma slammed into the island with all its might. Swirling, 150-mile winds brought destruction, tearing roofs off houses, upturning cars, tossing boats, snapping power lines, and stripping the leaves from trees.

When the tempest finally blew back out to sea, the 5,000 people living in St. John, especially in the town of Cruz Bay, were completely cut off. They had no power, no phone service, and their homes were in ruin. The nearby National Park was now filled with broken trees, wrecked beaches, and damaged buildings. In the park's waters, more than 64 boats were either sunk or washed up and stranded on the shore.

But the people of St. John weren't alone. With help from the U.S. Navy, the National Guard, and a host of volunteers, they began to clean up the enormous mess. Yet, two weeks later, another powerful storm, Hurricane Maria, struck the nearby island of St. Croix. While this one didn't directly hit

St. John, the fierce wind and rain were strong enough to cause further destruction.

The park was in chaos. But many people came to lend a helping hand. For three months, workers from the National Park Service, the U.S. Fish and Wildlife Service, and the U.S. Forest Service, plus, volunteers from organizations like Friends of the Virgin Islands National Park, helped clean up the park. They cleared fallen trees, rebuilt houses for park employees, and repaired other important historical structures. Finally, 105 long, hard days after Hurricane Irma touched down, the park re-opened to the public.

Today, the island looks a little different than the days before the hurricane. But many new businesses have bloomed, and though the losses are not forgotten, the residents are moving forward. The park has fared even better. Most of its major attractions have sprung back to life. Once again hikers can trek through the leafy forest on the Reef Bay Trail and, ultimately, end up on a beautiful white sand beach to laze in the sun. The reef fish of Trunk Bay's underwater snorkel trail beckon eager swimmers, and the campground in Cinnamon Bay is waiting for adventurers to pitch a tent and take in the stars.

The hurricane was devastating, no doubt. But the island's story shows that when people unite, they can achieve amazing things. It also reveals a lesson from nature—with time, life returns, and wounds heal.

The Solitary Mountain Man

Lake Clark National Park and Preserve, Alaska

Imagine living alone in nature for 30 years! An adventurer named Richard "Dick" Proenneke did just that when he set up home in a remote, roadless corner of Alaska. This is a land of snow-capped volcanoes, massive brown bears, and lakes so brilliantly blue.

Dick grew up on a farm in Iowa. He was very smart but quit high school to become a sailor in the U.S. Navy. Two years later, he contracted a serious illness that left him sick in bed for six long months. When Dick finally recovered, a wild idea took root in his adventurous heart. He decided that he wanted to live a life like no other. He spent years working in different trades, and in 1950 he moved to Alaska. Here he honed his skills in carpentry, operating and fixing machines, and fishing. All the while, he kept a lookout for the perfect spot to call home.

In 1967, at the age of 51, all alone and surrounded by towering peaks on the rugged northern shoreline of Twin Lakes, Dick began building his cabin. He harvested spruce trees by hand and notched the logs together to create an airtight home. He built a fireplace from nearby stones.

To keep fruits and vegetables from his garden fresh and cool, Dick buried metal containers deep into the ground. And sometimes friends flew in on float planes with treats like bacon, eggs, and hot chocolate. Life was good.

Dick loved Alaska and lived by one simple rule: his presence wouldn't harm the surrounding wilderness. He documented his life by writing in journals, taking photographs, and filming his life and work alone in the wild. These records eventually became a book, and later, a movie.

In 1980, almost two decades after he arrived, Lake Clark National Park was established, and Dick's cabin home became a part of it. Much of the park was protected from further development—preserving this natural wilderness for future generations.

At the age of 82, Dick bid Alaska farewell, settling in California where he lived the rest of his life. He left the National Park Service a precious parting gift—his cabin, which remains beautifully preserved today, whispering tales of a man who lived in harmony with nature.

The Big Bears

Katmai National Park and Preserve, Alaska

Mirror, mirror on the wall, who is the biggest bear of all? Every fall the rangers at Katmai National Park and Preserve answer this question with a playful tournament they call "Fat Bear Week." Using the park's live video camera, people from around the world vote on the heftiest bear. One year, a giant 1,400-pound bear named "747" (named after a jumbo jet), won the title!

The rangers celebrate the bears' weighty successes because these magnificent animals need the extra fat to survive the coming winter, when they'll spend the season hibernating. During this time, they eat and drink nothing and can shed up to one-third of their body weight. Come springtime, the bears crawl out of their dens and start fattening up all over again.

But how do they get so big? The park they call home sits on a mountainous peninsula that juts out into the Gulf of Alaska. Rivers rush from giant lakes into the sea. It is the perfect place for sockeye salmon, a fish with tasty pink meat that the brown bears love. Every summer, the sockeye make a long, perilous journey, swimming against the current, all the way upriver to the lake of their birth for a special mission—to lay their eggs, or spawn.

Before the salmon can reach the lake, they encounter an enormous barrier—a six-foot cascade known as Brooks Falls. But that's not all . . . clever brown bears await them! The bears are so smart that when the salmon arrive at the Falls in June, all they need to do is stand at the top with their mouths wide open. The fish, who are using all their strength to swim up and over the falls, leap, and if they're unlucky, land right into the bears' hungry mouths! It's a wild, watery dance of survival in the world of Katmai.

Keepers of the Light

Isle Royale National Park, Michigan

Though secluded and hard to reach, Isle Royale National Park is a place brimming with stories. This archipelago (cluster of islands) is made up of one giant 50-mile-long island (Isle Royale) surrounded by 450 smaller islands. It sits in the northwest corner of remote Lake Superior—the largest body of fresh water by surface area on the entire planet.

Bordered by Minnesota, Wisconsin, Michigan, and Ontario in Canada, Lake Superior is as big as the states of Vermont, Massachusetts, Rhode Island, Connecticut, and

New Hampshire combined! Its waters are so cold that the average annual temperature is 40° F. It is barely warm enough to dip a toe into, let alone swim for more than a few minutes.

To simply reach Isle Royale is an adventure. The only way in and out is by ferry, private boat, or float plane. Because Lake Superior is very dangerous in the winter, the park is open only from April to October. As a result, it's the least-visited national park in the lower 48 United States—with about 20,000 visitors per year.

Isle Royale may be remote, but its forests, thick with pine and open patches of blueberries, was inhabited 4,500 years ago by the Ojibwe people. They called this archipelago Minong. The meaning of the word is believed to have come from the words "Meen-oong," or "the good place," in tribute to its copper rich lands. The Ojibwe mined the metal to create tools, ornaments, and charms to keep them safe from harm. To extract the metal, the skilled miners would beat the bedrock with rounded stones from the shores of the lake. Ancient pottery and tools found throughout the park help piece together the stories of their way of life. Today, the Ojibwe still have hunting and gathering rights to these islands. They also travel to the park for important spiritual ceremonies.

Rock Harbor Lighthouse

Passage Island Lighthouse

Isle Royale Lighthouse

Rock of Ages Lighthouse

In the 1800s, as the region developed, shipping on Lake Superior increased. Isle Royale, which was surrounded by shallow rocky reefs posed an almost impossible challenge for passing ships. To reach their Canadian destination of Port Arthur, ships coming from the east would have to "thread the needle" between Passage Island and Blake Point, the easternmost point on the main island. Many of the voyages ended in a shipwreck.

To help the ships better navigate these treacherous waters, the U.S. government built four lighthouses around Isle Royale. Only one of them is on the main island. The other three sit on rocky islets far offshore. It's hard to imagine the solitude the lighthouse keepers must have felt, isolated for half the year, from May to December in this distant rocky realm. Some brought their families to relieve the loneliness and share in the beauty of the archipelago.

John Henry Malone, the keeper of Menagerie Island's Isle Royale Lighthouse, and his wife Julia Shea, raised 11 children on the remote nubbin of rock only a few hundred feet wide. To survive, they kept cows, ate seagull eggs, fished, and grew a garden. One year, in November, the ice around the island was so thick that John Malone compared it to living at the North Pole!

Of all the heroic lighthouse keepers these islands have seen, perhaps the bravest was John Soldenski. On a foggy day in May 1933, the steamship *George M. Cox*, loaded with passengers and an eight-piece orchestra, was celebrating its maiden voyage. A crash echoed! It had struck a reef near Isle Royale's Rock of Ages Lighthouse, right in the middle of the passengers' dinner. Swiftly, John Soldenski motored his boat out to the wreck. He towed the passengers in the ship's lifeboats back to the lighthouse, which stood on a pile of rocks near the northwest tip of Isle Royale. The lighthouse was so small that the wreck's 125 survivors had to take turns going inside to drink the warming coffee John's wife had prepared. Happily, everyone survived.

Today, the waters off Isle Royale are home to the National Park Service's most intact collection of shipwrecks, featuring ten major wrecks that span the course of 70 years, from the remains of massive freighters to wooden passenger steamers like the *George M. Cox*.

Sled Dogs to the Rescue

Denali National Park and Preserve, Alaska

More than 100 years ago, a man named Henry "Harry" Karstens stepped into the wild wonders of the brand-new Mount McKinley National Park. With him, he brought seven unruly, 14-month-old puppies. Harry, the park's first superintendent, had an enormous job ahead of him: marking park boundaries, building cabins, and protecting the wildlife from gold miners who were killing sheep and caribou to feed their workers. What good would seven lively puppies do?

But these weren't just any puppies, they were Alaskan sled dogs, destined to become legends. In 1922, when Harry bought the dogs, he paid $45 for each one. Today, that's almost $800 per dog! These pups were worth it. Growing sturdy and strong, they helped Harry haul timber, break trail, and track down the poachers who were killing wildlife.

Harry Kartsens was famous in his lifetime for being one of the first people to successfully climb Mount Denali in 1913. This feat as well as his knowledge of the area and skills got him the superintendent job.

Harry wasn't the first to rely on dogs in this way. For centuries, Indigenous peoples in the rugged, mountainous terrain of what is now Alaska have used teams of dogs for transportation. Alaskan sled dogs, which are traditionally bred from Samoyeds, Alaskan Malamutes, Siberian Huskies, and others, can be black and white, pure white, a rich caramel color, or any shade in between.

Today, about 30 dogs live in the park each equipped for their snowy adventures. With long legs to break through deep snow, compact paws that stop ice from building up between their toes, and sturdy fur coats, these pups can endure freezing temperatures. Their big, bushy tails wrap around their faces to stay warm. Perhaps their most impressive and useful traits include their love for humans, fellow dogs, and the thrill of pulling sleds through the wilderness, navigating the deep snow and fierce winds. On top of all this, they are intelligent and wonderful companions.

In 2015 President Barack Obama changed the name of Mount McKinley National Park to Denali National Park. The name comes from Koyukon, a traditional Native Alaskan language and means "tall one" because the park is home to 20,310-foot Denali, the highest mountain in North America. While the name may have changed, the sled dogs have been constant. Since Harry Karstens brought the first sled dogs to the park, it has operated a kennel, the only one in any U.S. National Park. Guests can visit the dogs at the kennel, which sits about three miles inside the park at Park Headquarters, or, from afar, people can watch new litters of puppies play on the park's webcam.

During the winter, the dogs are hard at work. Two million of the park's six million acres are wilderness, and motorized vehicles are not allowed. So the sled dog teams become the rangers' guiding lights, navigating to remote patrol cabins and transporting scientists to distant corners of the park. With their friendly, loving, often goofy nature, the dogs act as Denali's best ambassadors, bringing joy to this snowy paradise.

The Flight of the California Condor

Pinnacles National Park, California

In Pinnacles National park, lives a bird with a peculiar appearance—the California condor. With jet black feathers, a pink-orange head, a hooked beak, and beady eyes, these birds may not be beautiful, but oh can they soar! With wings that span almost ten feet, California condors race in the sky, covering up to 200 miles in a single day. But what makes them truly special is their role as Mother Nature's clean-up crew.

These scavengers have an unconventional diet. From poor ground squirrels squashed by cars to mighty whales washed ashore, they feast on the remains of the fallen. It might sound icky, but in nature's grand plan they play a crucial role.

Once, these magnificent birds ranged far and wide, from Baja California to British Columbia. But they were also rare because the female lays only one egg at a time. Both parents take turns warming the egg until it hatches and caring for the chick for the first six months of its life. The mother bird then takes two years to lay her next egg. This slow process means it takes time for condor numbers to grow. But it's not the only reason these birds are so rare . . .

During the 1900s, condors started to disappear altogether! The reason? Much of the dead carrion that the birds eat is killed by hunters, and the meat is poisoned by the lead in the hunter's bullets. In 1967, the California condor became an endangered species in the United States.

By the 1980s, only 22 condors remained.

Pinnacles National Parks became the perfect place for the birds to revive. Formed from volcanic activity that took place 23 million years ago, the park has very, very old rocks sculpted by wind and water, creating crags and spires that look like chubby fingers reaching into the sky. The tallest mountain in the park, North Chalone Peak offers the perfect ridgelines for birds to catch air currents so they can soar. They even nest in the cavities of the park's craggy rocks.

Pinnacles is the only park in the United States that is a release site for captive California condors. Park biologists welcome young birds from nearby zoos. First, the babies are put in a pen in the park to get comfortable with their surroundings. Then the scientists attach a radio transmitter and identification tag to each bird so they can keep track of them as they fly and roost throughout the park. The scientists monitor the birds closely, ensuring they have enough to eat and checking their blood for lead poisoning. When the birds are old enough to mate, the scientists even climb the craggy rocks into the birds' nest to monitor each new chick's health.

Tracking these enormous birds is hard work, but the scientists' persistence has paid off. The latest count reveals more than 500 California condors in the world, over 300 of which are flying in the wild.

The Spectacular Night Sky

Big Bend National Park, Texas

Bright lights are exciting. When the sun sets, the world's towns and cities shine in the dark. But this dazzling brilliance has an unintended consequence: it is making it harder for humans to see the natural night sky. Astronomers call this hazy phenomenon "luminous fog." Today, more than eighty percent of us live under light-polluted skies.

There are a few places, however, where the night sky remains untouched. Big Bend National Park in far west Texas is one of these places. Many miles away from any big city, it has the least light pollution of any national park in the Lower 48 states. On a clear night here, 2,000 stars can be seen twinkling in the inky blackness above, compared to only a few hundred in any medium-sized city.

Ancient peoples who lived and passed through this mountainous Chihuahuan Desert region, relied on the stars to navigate, predict seasonal changes, and for spiritual guidance. They wove stars into their stories, which they passed down to their children.

Today, visitors can still gaze into a universe of stars at Big Bend. Park officials have worked hard to preserve the visibility of the night sky by using less-polluting lights and using them only when necessary.

That means, when stargazers look up into the night sky here, in addition to the stars, they might even see a constellation, a planet, a meteor shower, or the brilliant shining array of the Milky Way galaxy.

The Bransfords of Mammoth Cave
Mammoth Cave National Park, Kentucky

Imagine exploring a vast underground universe that stretches from New York City to Washington, D.C. and back again. Speleologists (scientists who study caves) have done just that in Kentucky's Mammoth Cave, the world's longest-known underground cavern. It is currently mapped at 426 miles, but experts estimate that Mammoth could extend a total of 1,000 miles.

Humans began exploring Mammoth more than 4,000 years ago, when prehistoric Indigenous peoples mined it for precious minerals. The limestone cavern was rediscovered at the turn of the 19th century and became a wildly popular tourist attraction. Brave men like Materson "Mat" Bransford, an enslaved guide, explored the cave and led tourists by the light of kerosene lamps. Later, Mat's son,

Henry, joined him as a tour guide in the cave, too. When the family gained their freedom in the 1860s, the father and son continued to work as paid guides in Mammoth.

Henry's sons Matt and Louis also followed in their footsteps, guiding visitors, and opening a lodging house for Black visitors, to make sure they had the chance to experience the marvelous cavern. In 1941, as the cave became a national park, the Bransford family, who had lived in the area for more than a century, were forced off their land and the park didn't hire any Black guides. But the family never forgot the cave. In 2004, Jerry Bransford—Mat's great-great-grandson—returned to continue his family's work. Jerry guides new visitors and tells the tales of his ancestors, keeping their stories alive.

Fire!

Acadia National Park, Maine

On a map, the two islands that make up most of Acadia National Park look like opposing pincers on a giant lobster claw fishing for sea urchins in the Atlantic Ocean. Long before the park's creation, people have been drawn here . . .

Many years ago, these lands were the cherished home of four tribes known as the Wabanaki or "people of the dawn." These four tribes, the Maliseet, Micmac, Penobscot, and Passamaquoddy, have been hunting, fishing, and digging for clams here for 12,000 years. Even today, their descendants carry on ancient traditions, skilfully harvesting sweetgrass and ash to weave beautiful baskets.

As the United States developed, colonizers from Europe arrived, bringing disease and war to the original inhabitants. Many Indigenous peoples were killed or forced away, but others resisted and remained. Still, European settlers like Irishman John Carroll who arrived in the 1800s carved out homesteads in what is now the park. The Carrolls lived here for three generations, and the family's homestead still stands to illustrate one of many chapters in the park's history.

In the mid-1800s, artists found this rugged landscape of mountains, forests, and rocky coastline. Their paintings drew tourists to the islands. Before Acadia National Park was founded in 1919, the wealthy philanthropist John D. Rockefeller, Jr., wanted to explore the woods and rocky peaks on horseback, so he funded the construction of 45 miles of carriage roads. These stone pathways were built to stand the test of time, but were also beautifully ornate, with arched stone bridges that spanned rivers and overlooked waterfalls. This peaceful oasis became a place for visitors to escape the frantic pace of life in big cities like Boston and New York. Until disaster struck the park in 1947 in the form of a mysterious fire.

After an unusually dry summer, on October 17 1947, a local resident spotted smoke rising from a nearby cranberry bog. No one knows how the fire began, but no matter the cause, the blaze quickly spread, with flames fanned by high winds that frequently shifted direction.

For centuries, Indigenous peoples, including those from across the United States, have used fire as a tool to manage the landscape. This practice is known as "cultural burning" where small, frequent, and controlled fires are set to burn off brush and trees. This improves the habitat for animals, medicinal plants, and foods like blueberries. But the fire that burned in Maine in the autumn of 1947, was not a careful incident of cultural burning. It was an accident that quickly spiraled into an out-of-control disaster.

Firefighters from around the country, including the Army Air Corps, the Navy, the Coast Guard, and National Park Service employees from other parks around the East, rallied to join the local fire crews to battle the blaze.

Even with so many helping hands, the fire continued to spread. In just one week 2,300 acres had burned. The blaze was quickly heading toward the town of Bar Harbor, an important place for the Wabanaki peoples, historically known as "Moneskatik," or "the clam digging place." In less than three hours, the fire engulfed houses, hotels, and businesses in Bar Harbor. As the fire raged around them, residents were forced to escape by sea and by car, navigating through a tunnel of smoke and debris to safety.

Finally, ten days after it started, on October 27, the fire was declared under control. By the time it was out, nearly one-fifth of Acadia National Park lay in ruins. Tragically, a few lives were lost and no one knows how many animals died as well.

It took months for work crews to clear the charred landscape. Yet, almost a century later, Acadia's forest thrives. Seeds carried on the wind turned into beautiful new stands of birch and aspen, which eventually gave way to spruce and fir, ultimately creating a stronger, more diverse forest than before the fire. It was a terrifying disaster for residents, but today, the fire is the reason that Acadia's forest is so healthy. Now, new generations are able to delight in the deciduous trees that flame so brilliantly red, orange, and yellow every fall.

The Supernatural Powers of the Ancient Redwood

Redwood National Park, California

In northern California's Redwood National Park there stands a tree called Hyperion. It reaches twice the height of the Statue of Liberty, soaring an incredible 379 feet into the sky. Discovered by tall tree experts Chris Atkins and Michael Taylor in 2006, Hyperion became the record-holder of the tallest tree known in the world. It is a true giant among giants!

Hyperion is a Coast Redwood, part of a special family of trees that includes, the Dawn Redwood in China and the Giant Sequoia in the Sierra Nevada mountains. However, none can match the magnificent height of the Coast Redwood. These trees can grow and grow thanks to the abundant rain and nutrient-rich soil of its coastal home.

Standing proud, it wears a coat of rough, reddish-brown bark, with a crown of vibrant green branches with feathery needles. But these trees are not only giants, they are ancient beings. Hyperion is estimated to be between 600 and 800 years old, holding many secrets whispered through the wind over time.

Hyperion's exact location remains a secret so that it may live and grow in peace. In its hidden realm, between northern California and southern Oregon, 60 to 140 inches of rain falls per year. The heavy fog that drifts from the Pacific Ocean keeps the air moist, helping the trees reach for the sky and the plants below grow. The secret to the Coast Redwood's long life is that it has almost supernatural powers, defending against a trio of tree destroyers: insects, fungi, and fire.

The tree fights off bugs and fungi because it makes a chemical called tannin in its bark. Tannin gives the tree its red color and makes it unappealing for insects and fungi that want to eat or live on it. Another cool thing about tannin is that if a branch falls off, the tannin covers the broken end of the tree like a bandage, protecting it from decay. The Coast Redwood is also more resistant to fire than other trees. That's because it contains no pitch or resin, the highly flammable, sticky substance that oozes out of pine and fir trees.

Redwood National Park, with its four surrounding state parks stands as a sanctuary by preserving almost half of the world's remaining old-growth Coast Redwoods. Here, the mighty Smith River flows freely filled with salmon and steelhead trout. Miles of trails weave through the forest, leading down to Pacific Ocean tidal pools filled with sea stars, crabs, and anemones.

But, it is the towering, majestic, trees that steal the spotlight, their branches creating a wonderful canopy where visitors walk beneath, or even drive through their trunks. Every step reveals an experience many visitors will never forget.

The Slow-Motion Sea Cow

Everglades National Park, Florida

Down in the shallow, slow-moving waters of southern Florida, something peculiar swims. Meet the West Indian manatee, or the "Sea Cow". This remarkable mammal weighs around 1,000 pounds and stretches ten feet long. With its gray, wrinkled skin and large flippers, it peacefully grazes on seagrasses under the warm Florida sun in Everglades National Park. And it is one of the most beloved marine mammals in the Sunshine State.

Everglades National Park is a universe of both fresh- and saltwater—a giant, slow-moving system of rivers lined by mangroves, swamps, sawgrass marshes, and flatwood forests. It is the largest subtropical wilderness in the United States and the only place in the world where American crocodiles and alligators coexist.

Other animal residents include schools of playful dolphins, the endangered Florida panther, and 350 species of colorful birds like the pink-feathered Roseate spoonbill.

Among all this interesting wildlife, the Florida manatee holds a special place in peoples' hearts. It's not just its gentle nature that makes it so beloved, but it is also its intelligence. Similar to elephants, manatees have a remarkable long-term memory, allowing them to migrate hundreds of miles to familiar warm-water spots. To communicate, they use a language of touch, squeals, squeaks, and chirps. That's how a mama manatee stays in touch with her baby.

These animals have special skills, too. Florida manatees come up for air once every five or so minutes but can stay underwater for twenty minutes if needed. They swim by waving their mermaid-like tails, and interestingly they don't have necks, so they turn their entire body to look around. Their average lifespan is about 30 years in the wild, but Snooty, a famous manatee who lived at the Bishop Museum of Science and Nature in Bradenton, Florida, lived to be 69! Over the course of his lifetime, Snooty greeted more than a million visitors and helped shape humans' understanding of and love for his species.

Sadly, these wonderful creatures almost went extinct in the 1960s. Because Florida manatees are so slow-moving, they were an easy target for hunters. And their wide-ranging habitat, which includes rivers, bays, canals, estuaries, and coastal areas in fresh, salt, and brackish water, makes them vulnerable to getting injured by a motorboat's propeller. Finally, in 1967, the Florida manatee was listed as an endangered species. To tackle the problem, the state developed a Manatee Recovery Plan that helped bring its population back up. Manatees were finally taken off the endangered species list in 2017, but these friendly beasts are still considered vulnerable and need ongoing protection.

One of the reasons scientists and others are so concerned about the Florida manatees' ongoing survival is because they do not reproduce very quickly. Females carry their babies for 12 months—three months longer than humans—and give birth once every two years. They also face lots of other threats, including a shrinking number of shallow, warm springs due to pollution and human activities. These springs are a favorite manatee habitat. The poor creatures can also get tangled up in fishing gear, and go hungry because there is less and less seagrass, one of the foods they rely on.

It is estimated that there are between 7,000 to 8,000 manatees in the entire state of Florida. At Everglades National Park, at last count, scientists observed 176 adults and seven calves in park waters. Park biologists closely monitor their health and work tirelessly to protect these creatures.

Initiatives to protect the manatees include projects that restore seagrass, laws that control boat traffic and speed, and educational tours in the park that allow visitors to safely see these gentle giants and encourage them to learn more about these lovable creatures and how to protect them.

The Greatest Discovery

Badlands National Park, South Dakota

Deep in Badlands National Park, a curious seven-year-old explorer named Kylie Ferguson stumbled upon a dazzling discovery. It all happened during a Junior Ranger program in 2010 when Kylie noticed something shiny and white peeking out from a butte near the park's visitor center. Eager to share her find, she documented every detail and reported it to the park. It turned out to be the skull of a long-extinct Hoplophoneus—a catlike creature from the Nimravidae family that once roamed the Earth 25 to 39 million years ago!

The Badlands, with its wild, rolling landscape and pastel-colored buttes, is the ultimate fossil treasure trove. These buttes hold layers of rocks like a time machine, capturing the Earth's history over millions of years. They slowly built up and then gradually eroded away around 500,000 years ago. The rocks hold beautifully preserved ancient specimens, allowing us to journey back millions and millions of years!

In 1846, 132 years before Badlands became a national park, the first brontothere fossils were discovered. This plant eater was larger than a rhino and had blunt horns. It once inhabited the hot, lush forests that covered what is now the arid Badlands during the late Eocene epoch, which lasted from about 54.8 to 33.7 million years ago. Other remarkable finds include fragments of mosasaurs—gigantic marine lizards that lived during the time of the dinosaurs.

Kylie's saber-tooth cat discovery sparked the opening of the Fossil Preparation Lab in 2012. This is a paleontology lab and museum staffed by paleontologists, or scientists who study fossils. Here, visitors can watch these scientists at work as they carefully clean, analyze, and catalog the fossils that are found in the park. Every year, the lab receives hundreds of reports from visitors, some of which lead to important new findings. Fossils carry important clues that help scientists piece together the history of our planet.

It's not only long-gone creatures that can be found here. No, the park is a beautiful wilderness alive with all sorts of animals. Endangered black-footed ferrets skuttle about and majestic bighorn sheep proudly display their curly horns. The park is also home to the pronghorn, North America's fastest hoofed animal that can run up to sixty miles per hour. Amongst the grasses, visitors must watch their steps for slithering prairie rattlesnakes, and be sure to give the mighty American bison a wide berth. And as day turns to night, thousands of stars sparkle in the sky painting a breathtaking picture above this wondrous park.

The Unsung Little Sister

Capitol Reef National Park, Utah

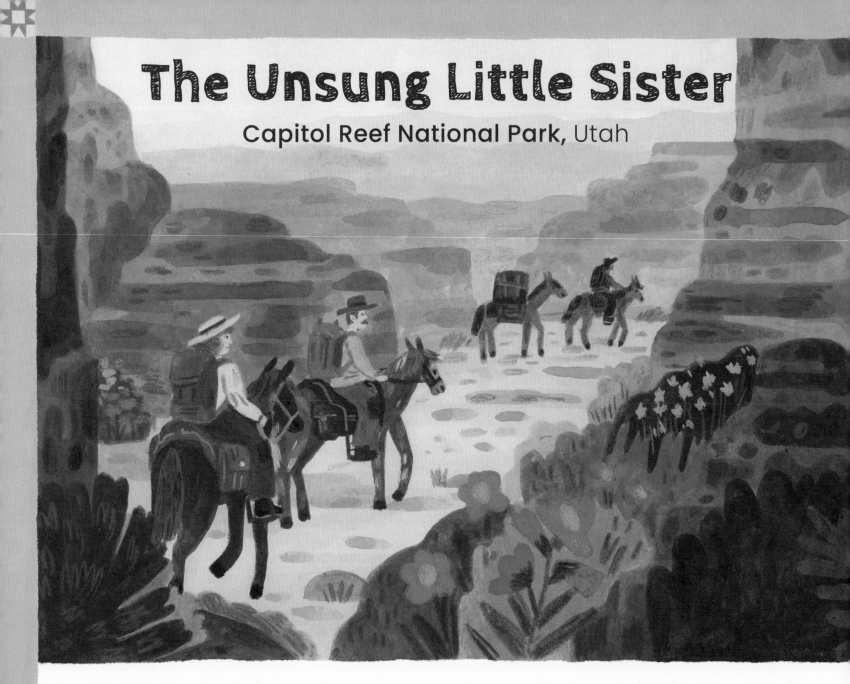

Every little sister or little brother knows that sometimes the older siblings get all the attention. This was especially true for a little sister called Ellen. Her big brother, Major John Wesley Powell, was famous for being a skilled geologist—a scientist who studies rocks. He was also a soldier who lost his right arm while fighting in the Civil War. Despite the loss of his arm, John was the first white man to successfully lead an expedition down the fierce rapids of the Colorado River between the towering cliffs of the Grand Canyon in 1869.

But Ellen was amazing in her own right. Back in the 1800s, not many girls went to college, but Ellen did. She became a schoolteacher when she was just 16 years old. Later, she became a botanist, which is a scientist who studies plants. She also worked hard to help women get the right to vote. In 1871 Ellen joined her husband Almon Thompson on a special expedition to explore one of last areas unmapped by the U.S. government (a region around the Utah and Arizona border). Ellen was the only woman on the trip, and she was tough! She wore men's clothes to sit astride her horse and rode for up to 20 miles a day. The expedition was difficult, traveling through deep snow and under a hot desert sun, but Ellen didn't give up.

During the expedition, Ellen collected hundreds of plant specimens, sending the dried, pressed plants back to a professor at Harvard University. Along the way, she made friends with and learned the language of the Southern

Paiute people who lived in southwestern Utah. Toward the end of the expedition the group reached what is now Capitol Reef National Park, a fascinating puzzle of rocks that have been warped, folded, and shifted over millions of years. One odd formation of Navajo sandstone domes reminded the explorers of the rotunda on the U.S. Capitol building. Other formations were steep, rocky cliffs that were hard to navigate like underwater reefs, and so they decided on the name "Capitol Reef."

Right as the expedition entered what is now the national park, Ellen was so exhausted that she decided to return to base camp early. But she still made history! Three plants she found were completely new to her fellow-

scientists back east. Today those plants are all named after her: Thompson's Woolly Milkvetch, Thompson's Dalea, and Thompson's Penstemon.

Ellen's adventures didn't stop there. Later in her life she moved to Washington D.C., where she joined the women's Suffragette movement. This movement wanted women to have the right to vote, and Ellen worked hard among other famous activists like Susan B. Anthony and Elizabeth Cady Stanton. Sadly, she didn't live to see Congress pass the 19th Amendement that gave women the right to vote in 1920, but her efforts helped make it happen. Ellen Powell Thompson may have been a little sister but she was also a true hero who helped change the world.

Welcome to the Wonderful Watery Underworld

Biscayne National Park, Florida

Most national parks are on land—wild woods, rugged mountains, colorful meadows. And the wildlife within them is often fierce and impressive, from bison in Grand Teton to wolves in Yellowstone. But not all parks follow this pattern . . . Within sights of Miami—a bustling city, home to six million people—is a secret, sprawling underwater world: Biscayne National Park. This endless wonderland of turquoise waters is filled with more fish species (over 600) than all the fish, bird, reptile, amphibian, and mammal species combined in Yellowstone National Park.

Beneath the tangy saltwater playful dolphins, flying fish, gentle manatees, and colorful reef fish dart and dance. Biscayne Park is a marine paradise where four different ecosystems meet: the mainland's mangrove forest, southern Biscayne Bay, the northernmost Florida Keys, and a section of the Florida Reef, the third-largest coral reef in the world.

But the story of how this watery paradise came to be is surprising. Some 10,000 years ago, during the last ice age, Biscayne Bay was once a dry, flat savanna. Ancient peoples roamed, hunting for mighty mammoths and mastodons. When the ice age finally ended, the land filled with water. It's likely that groups of Paleo Indians, the first peoples of what we now call North and South America, settled here. Many of their artifacts remain lost underwater, slowly unveiling through archaeological discoveries.

Time brought new settlers—people who learned to thrive by the water. One group known to have settled here were the Tequesta people. They were expertly skilled fisherfolk who understood the riches the sea offered. But when European colonizers arrived in the 16th century, they brought diseases such as smallpox and measles which killed many Indigenous people. By the mid 1700s, most of the original inhabitants were gone—either dead or forced away—their history buried beneath the growing nearby cities.

The story of this place didn't end there though. Over the years, a few modern settlers set up home, like "Crawfish" Eddie Walker. He built the first shack in Stiltsville, a unique community of over-water buildings. In the 1930s, Crawfish Eddie, served lobster chowder from his shack to passing boaters. After the park was established in 1980, the last Stiltsville residents were forced to leave, and their homes were preserved as historical landmarks. Today, six buildings in Stiltsville still stand, all of which miraculously survived Hurricane Irma in 2017.

Down on the seabed, more of this park's past awaits. The underwater Maritime Heritage Trail which today's visitors can dive and snorkel along, features six shipwrecks from over the span of a century. One sunken treasure is the *Mandalay*, a double-masted sailing ship that ran aground on New Year's Day in 1966. And above water, the 130-feet-high Fowey Rocks Lighthouse, first lit in 1878, shines over the bay as "the eye of Miami."

As well as human stories, this glorious undersea realm is filled with wildlife. In Jones Lagoon's peaceful mangroves, visitors paddleboard on the calm, shallow waters—while beneath them, dainty looking Cassiopeia jellyfish, sea cucumbers, and sea stars swim and sway. And in the Florida Reef section of the park an entire living, coral city thrives.

Here, each of the fishy inhabitants, from blue neon gobies and yellow striped porkfish to clever octopuses and gentle nurse sharks, have their own tales to tell.

Biscayne National Park is a guardian of marine wonders, but also a keeper of the region's prehistoric past.

Light after Dark

Great Smoky Mountains National Park,
North Carolina and Tennessee

Sprawling across North Carolina and Tennessee, Great Smoky Mountains National Park stands as the most popular in the United States. It welcomes 13 million visitors each year. There is so much to see and do here, from hiking a portion of the 2,190-mile Appalachian Trail, to climbing to the 6,643-foot summit of Clingmans Dome, to learning about the fascinating plants and animals that live here, like the synchronous firefly.

The park today is full of sights and stories. But it also holds an important history. Long before Great Smoky Mountains became a national park, it was home to an entire nation of people, the Cherokee, who lived in this region for centuries. However, In the 1830s, the U.S. government forcibly removed the Cherokee to free up land for white farmers who wanted to grow cotton and other crops. About 17,000 Cherokee men, women, and children were marched across the Mississippi River to what is now Oklahoma and Arkansas. Many other Indigenous tribes faced the same fate. This brutal six-month, 1,200-mile journey is remembered as the "Trail of Tears" because of the devastation it caused. An estimated 6,000 Cherokee died from cold, hunger, and disease along the way.

About a century later, residents were forced to leave once more so that the new national park could be created in 1934. Many of these residents were sharecroppers (tenant farmers who don't own the lands they work), therefore they received no compensation for the farms and homes they had to leave behind. Many of the buildings they abandoned still stand in the park today.

These stories are not forgotten. And though people no longer live within the park, it is an important refuge for flora and fauna. Containing more than 20,000 species of plants and animals, Great Smoky Mountains has more biological diversity than any other national park in the U.S. The mountains burst into vibrant blooms, creating a natural rainbow on the hillsides, and animals thrive. Each member of this marvelous ecosystem has a story. One of the most interesting critters is the synchronous firefly, which is also known as a lightning bug, but is really a beetle!

This firefly is one of 19 species in the park but is one of the only kind in which the males can synchronize their flashing light patterns to attract females in a dazzling dance.

Synchronous fireflies produce light in the pale area of the abdomen known as their "lantern." They illuminate in a series of five to eight flashes, followed by a pause of about eight seconds, which keeps repeating as they fly. At first the flashing appears random, but as more males join in, the flashing begins to synchronize and entire sections of the forest light up!

This natural light production is called bioluminescence. Peak flash-dance season for the Synchronous firefly normally occurs over a two-week period starting in late May. But there are countless other natural wonders to explore in Great Smoky Mountains all year round.

Bat Ballet

Carlsbad Caverns National Park,
New Mexico

In a dry corner of southeastern New Mexico there's an entire underground universe known as Carlsbad Caverns. The 120 known caves in this system began to form four to six million years ago when water from below the Earth's surface that was rich in the chemical hydrogen sulfide, mixed with rainwater falling from above. Together, the waters created sulfuric acid that dissolved the limestone rock and created the caves.

The longest-known cave in this hidden underworld is Lechuguilla which stretches 145 miles into the dark. Then there's the 30-mile-long Carlsbad Cavern and its famous Big Room, the largest cave chamber in North America.

These caves aren't empty . . . creatures scuttle in the shadows. One of the most interesting residents that lives

inside Carlsbad Caverns is the Brazilian free-tailed bat, a tiny mammal weighing just a half-ounce. Hundreds of thousands of them live together in an enormous colony. Every evening from early spring and into the fall, the bats leave the cave to hunt insects. This mass exit is known as an "outflight." It's a mystery how the bats know when to leave the cave, but scientists have pinpointed their departure time to be "civil twilight," or about 28 minutes past sunset. Even more mysterious, when they leave the cave, the bats always spiral out of it in a counterclockwise direction. This precision performance looks like a massive bat ballet that can last up to three hours. It's a thrilling sight to behold!

The Fall of Prometheus
Great Basin National Park, Nevada

Great Basin National Park, isn't just a big valley; it's a place full of surprises. With 40 hidden caves and towering mountains like 13,065-feet Wheeler Peak, it is also home to a variety of animals. Here, rabbits scamper and majestic eagles swoop and soar.

In the lofty mountains are groves of bristlecone pines, the world's longest-living trees. These pines have gnarled, twisty trunks shaped by wind and ice. Short, dark green needles grow in tufts of five along the branches. The secret to these trees' long life is that their high, cold, and windy home makes them grow very slowly and their wood turns tough like armor. This keeps them safe from rot, fungi, insects, and erosion that can harm other trees.

Among these ancient trees, Prometheus stood as one of the oldest. In 1964, a research student got permission to cut into the tree to test its age. He discovered it was about 4,900 years old. Eventually, Prometheus died, but parts of its trunk remain in the park where visitors can stop and count its rings. But the story continues . . .

In 2012, scientists found an even older bristlecone that was a staggering 5,065 years old. And they think there could be even more ancient trees still to find. Park rangers are very protective of these trees and ask visitors not to take fallen bristlecone pine wood home because it could be thousands of years old and contain important secrets of history.

The Greatest Climb
Yosemite National Park, California

When Yosemite National Park was established in 1890, no one on Earth would have believed that a rock climber would be able to scale the sheer granite walls of El Capitan! This 3,600-foot-tall vertical rock formation rises straight up out of the western end of Yosemite Valley. It is one of the most famous rocks in the world. Flowing off its east side is Horsetail Falls, where every February a magical event occurs: The cascading water reflects the orange glow of the setting sun, and the entire waterfall appears to be on fire!

Before the first Europeans reached Yosemite Valley in 1851, the original peoples of this land—the Ahwahneechee—called El Capitan To-tock-ah-noo-lah, or "Rock Chief," because of the way it seemed to stand guard over this beautiful valley full of cascading waterfalls, rushing rivers, and dark green forest of giant sequoia trees.

In 1957, an adventurer named Warren Harding led an expedition to climb this seemingly unclimbable peak. To do so, his expedition crew drilled iron bolts and inserted metal pitons that would act as anchors to hold their ropes, up the entire face of the wall. Over the course of one year, it took 45 days to carefully climb to the summit. When the men reached the top, their achievement was heralded as one of the greatest ascents of all time.

Since Harding's expedition, hundreds of climbers have traced his steps to Yosemite National Park to attempt to climb El Capitan. Many have been successful. But none have attempted anything so dangerous and difficult as Alex Honnold. The young Californian grew up in the state capital of Sacramento and began rock climbing in a gym at the age of five. By the time he was ten, the tall and lean pre-teen was climbing almost every day. Alex eventually went to college to study civil engineering. But his passion was for rocks, not books. He left college behind to drive all over California in his mom's old van, chasing the sun so that he could camp out and climb magnificent rocks. Alex climbed and climbed, living out of his van for ten years at places like Yosemite National Park so that he could be as close to the rocks as he could possibly be.

Then on June 3, 2017, Alex achieved the unimaginable. He became the first person to climb El Capitan without any ropes or safety gear, relying only on his hands and feet. This kind of climbing is called "free solo" and is very dangerous. It takes enormous concentration and courage, and should only be attempted by those who are already very skilled rock climbers. Alex completed the 2,900-foot route in three hours and fifty-six minutes, an astonishing world record.

Though dangerous, Alex's climb inspired many people around the world. His own mother, Dierdre Wolownick, started rock climbing at the age of 60. Six years later, she became the oldest woman to climb El Capitan (using safety ropes). Four years later, she broke her own record at the age of 70. Each climber who faces El Capitan shows the world that even the mightiest rocks can be conquered by those with the spirit to reach for the heights.

A Hazardous Journey
Mount Rainier National Park, Washington

Wildflower meadows, ancient forests, rushing rivers, and waterfalls—these are just a few of the natural treasures to be found in Mount Rainier National Park. Visitors flock to take in the iconic scenery and catch a glimpse of the park's wildlife. Garter snakes slither underfoot in the summer, colorful harlequin ducks paddle, and a range of mammals rove the land, including Cascade red foxes and black bears. Even rare wolverines were spotted here in 2020. But perhaps the biggest draw of all is the great mountain itself.

Mount Rainier is a glorious, scary peak to climb. Rising 14,410 feet, like a giant guardian in the Cascade Mountain Range. It's not just any mountain, it's a colossal active volcano wearing a snowy crown. From faraway in Seattle, it looms so large that it feels almost touchable. The snow-capped peak, with glaciers flowing off its flanks, is the crown jewel of Rainier National Park.

This mountain holds a fascinating story—it's a stratovolcano, a mountain made of layers of lava and ash. Way, way back, almost a half a million years ago, long before humans lived here, Mount Rainer shook the earth with powerful eruptions. One was so powerful that it created enormous rivers of water, rocks, and dirt that flowed down from the summit. And an eruption 5,600 years ago was so explosive that it moved 130 billion cubic feet of debris. This is enough to bury a whole area the size of Manhattan under tons of mud and rocks!

Now, Mount Rainier hasn't erupted in more than 150 years, but scientists believe the volcano is the most dangerous in the Cascade Mountain Range for three reasons. First, it is so tall that when it erupts, the debris that explodes out of the crater can fly really far. Second, it sits on two shifting tectonic plates, making the mountain shake with lots of tiny earthquakes—hundreds every year. Finally, there are more than 20 glaciers near the summit that could melt in hot lava.

Indigenous peoples have lived near Mount Rainier for centuries, learning and using its meadows and forested slopes to hunt and gather food and other resources. But they have also been mindful of the mountain's power. In the summer of 1870, three non-native mountaineers, Americans P.B. Van Trump, his friend General Hazard Stevens, and an Englishman named Edmund T. Coleman, set out to climb the peak with the help and expertise of a Yakama Indian guide named Sluiskin.

The going was rough, and the men were carrying very heavy packs with frames made of wood and leather. Coleman was so miserable that he turned around before the team even reached the first plateau. Van Trump, Stevens, and Sluiskin pushed on to the tree line. This is the point on the mountain where trees stop growing and the rest of the way up is just snow and ice and deep crevasses. Sluiskin, who believed that evil spirits lived beyond that point, told the two men that he would go no farther.

On the ninth day of their climb, in raging winds and bitter cold, Stevens and Van Trump finally reached what they thought was the summit. They started to celebrate . . . until they turned around and saw that they had not reached the top. Mount Rainier's true summit loomed 250 feet higher. The sun was setting and the wind was howling, so the men could climb no more. Instead, they followed the rim of a snow-filled crater, where Van Trump saw steam rising out from a crack. The two men wedged into the crack, which opened into a cave that had been formed by steam coming from deep within the volcano, melting the ice down to the rock layer below. Van Trump and Stevens tried to rest, wondering if they would be alive by morning.

Early the next day, they were thankfully alive. However, they were shivering and sick to their stomachs from sulfur. This is a chemical that smells like rotten eggs and is often found in volcanoes. The men quickly hurried to the top where they left behind their water canteen and a brass plate with their names embossed on it as proof of their presence.

The men made it down the mountain successfully, but not everyone believed that they had truly conquered this seemingly unconquerable peak. Two months later, another expedition team on a quest to the summit, found a rope the men had used to cross a crevasse near the summit. But to this day, no one has ever found the canteen and brass plate they left at the top.

A mere twenty years later, in 1890, Fay Fuller, became the first woman to reach Mount Rainier's summit. In 1899, Rainier became the United States' fifth national park and Van Trump was its first ranger. He fought for years to reinstate the mountain's original Indigenous name, "Takoma," but his request was never granted. More than 150 years after Van Trump and Stevens's climb, Mount Rainier has become such a popular peak that close to 10,000 climbers set out to reach its summit each year.

The Long Journey of the Leatherback

Dry Tortugas National Park, Florida

In the middle of the Gulf of Mexico, there's a special place called Tortugas National Park. Picture seven small islands, like tiny tropical secrets, surrounded by clear blue waters. The biggest of these islands is only 49 acres, roughly the size of 38 football fields. These islands, though small, and mostly wild today, once played a mighty important role in U.S. history . . .

In the 1800s, Garden Key—the main island—was home to Fort Jefferson, a fortress shaped like a giant hexagon. It stood guard against pirates and invaders along the southern coast. It was one of the country's biggest forts. But after just 40 years, hurricanes and outbreaks of yellow fever forced the army to abandon it in 1874.

Nowadays, these pancake-flat, yellow-sand ringed islands play another very important role. They are a safe haven for a very special group of creatures— the sea turtles. Five species live in these waters: the Green, Loggerhead, Kemp's Ridley, Hawksbill, and Leatherback. They are all endangered.

Leatherback
Sea Turtle

Hawksbill
Sea Turtle

Loggerhead
Sea Turtle

Kemp's Ridley
Sea Turtle

Green Sea
Turtle

The largest turtle of them all is the leatherback. It doesn't have a hard shell like the others; instead, it wears tough, rubbery skin (carapace) with seven ridges (keels). These turtles can grow to be as heavy as 2,000 pounds and are incredible divers. They can plunge 4,000 feet down, as deep as many whales, and stay underwater for 85 minutes. But the most amazing thing about leatherbacks is their epic journeys. They can swim up to 10,000 miles in a single year. The life of a leatherback is itself one long journey. Tiny chicks hatch on moonlit beaches and crawl to the ocean where they spend the rest of their lives migrating between their breeding and feeding areas.

In the past, leatherbacks were plentiful in every ocean across the planet except the icy Arctic and Antarctic waters. But their numbers are dwindling fast, especially in the Pacific Ocean. Sadly, leatherbacks get caught up in fishing lines and nets, people hunt them for their meat and their eggs, and sometimes, the turtles mistake harmful plastic for jelly fish and eat it.

Only one in a thousand leatherback hatchlings survive to adulthood. But there is a glimmer of hope: the leatherbacks swimming near Dry Tortugas, seem to be doing better. Scientists and conservation organizations worldwide are on a mission to protect these magnificent, ancient reptiles whose roots can be traced to a turtle family that has been around for more than 100 million years.

The Pioneering Park Ranger

Grand Canyon National Park, Arizona

When Polly Mead graduated from the prestigious University of Chicago in 1928, her wealthy aunt gave her the choice between two gifts. She could either embark on a European adventure or return to Grand Canyon National Park in Arizona to dive deeper into her love for botany. Her heart was already captured by the Grand Canyon's breathtaking beauty during a school field trip in 1927, so her decision was swift—back to the Grand Canyon she went.

One mile deep, 277 miles long, and about ten miles wide from rim to rim, the Grand Canyon reveals rock that formed an astonishing 1.8 billion years ago. The canyon itself is relatively young, carved by the mighty Colorado River about five to six million years ago. It's an exhilarating place that fills hearts with wonder—mighty bison and bighorn sheep roam the land, peregrine falcons and Mexican spotted owls soar through the sky, snakes, scorpions, and insects scurry through the undergrowth and hardy, striking plants bloom across the landscape.

Polly spent two summers after college researching the plants of the canyon's north rim. She was no stranger to the outdoors. One of eight siblings, she grew up in Colorado and would embark on overnight trips deep into the park. She would bring only three things on these trips: a bedroll (like an old-fashioned sleeping bag), a plant press to protect her plant specimens, and a pistol for safety.

Polly loved her work so much that she applied for a position with the U.S. Forest Service as a naturalist. But her request was denied since they did not hire female naturalists at the time. Polly would not give up. She tried again, this time through the National Park Service in 1930, and she succeeded! She became Grand Canyon National Park's first female ranger-naturalist and only the second-ever in the entire National Park Service.

Back then, there were so few women in the National Park Service that there was no uniform for Polly to wear. So, she wore the clothes she used for riding horses. Instead of a Stetson cowboy hat, she wore a floppy felt hat, fashionable for women at the time.

For two years, Polly guided hikes of the canyon's South Rim, planted wildflower gardens, delivered campfire lectures, led car tours, and continued her research and writing on the botany of the area. Unofficially, she also inspired many young girls who realized that maybe one day they, too, could follow in her footsteps and become naturalists like her.

Polly married Preston P. Patraw, the park's assistant superintendent and, as was common in those days, she left her job to become a housewife, traveling with her husband as he climbed the ladder of his career at various parks.

In 1954, more than 20 years after she left, Polly finally returned to Grand Canyon National Park when her husband became Superintendent. By then she was a superstar in her own right. In 1952, she published *Flowers of the Southwest Mesas*, a book filled with detailed drawings and descriptions of hundreds of flowering plants. It was a marvelous success, selling 65,000 copies and establishing the trailblazing, one-time park ranger as the top expert on the flora of Grand Canyon National Park.

School of Rock
Arches National Park, Utah

In the heart of Utah, lies a red rock wonderland, where time, water, and salt have forged a geographical marvel: Arches National Park. People come from far and wide to see these soaring red rock arches, fins, pinnacles, and strangely shaped rocks.

Sitting high on the Colorado Plateau above the Colorado River, the park is a treasure trove of over 2,000 rock arches and among them, the most famous is Delicate Arch. Despite standing for millions of years, this 46-foot-high ancient rock arch appears as if a gentle breeze or the slightest touch could tip it over. And then, there's Landscape Arch— an immense natural structure, stretching longer than any other arch in North America.

In this place, where nature has shaped such dazzling rock formations, is a world of wildlife. Eagles and hawks decorate the clear blue skies, looking for prey. Mule deer, with their long ears and white tails, wander quietly among the rocks. Smaller animals like rabbits and lizards dart in and out of the crevices, making this land their home.

But a long, long time ago—more than 300 million years ago—this place was very different. It used to be a large, shallow bay that was part of a big ocean. The weather was hot and dry, and as the water slowly evaporated and disappeared, it left behind salt deposits. Over many, many thousands of years, layers of sediments and dirt covered the salt, and it turned into rock too. The rock was squished and bent, wrinkled and warped by powerful forces in the Earth.

Down below, the salt, which was softer and more flexible than the rock above, started pushing its way up. Massive bumps began to form beneath a thin layer of rock.

Slowly, all the land began to rise far, far above sea level, and wind and water started to carve away at the rock.

When the rock layers that covered the salt were finally revealed, they began to twist and crack. Rainwater trickled down, dissolving the salt and shaping the rocks into long narrow fins. And the rocks eventually turned into the beautiful arches we see today.

It would take years to try to find all 2,000 arches, but some, like Delicate Arch, are right there along the main road for everyone to see. These rocks remind us that our time on Earth is just a tiny part of the grand story of our planet.

Where the Buffalo Roam
Theodore Roosevelt National Park, North Dakota

In the rolling prairies and pastel-colored hills of Theodore Roosevelt National Park, alongside the wild horses and golden eagles, lives a creature larger than a polar bear. It is a true powerhouse called the American bison. This mighty beast, weighing up to 2,000 pounds, stands tall at six feet and can sprint at an astonishing 35 miles per hour. Its head, covered with long, wiry fur, is so powerful that it can push aside mounds of snow to forage for hidden plants beneath to eat. And when a bison gets angry, its tail shoots straight up like an arrow, warning it could charge at any moment!

In prehistoric times, millions of American bison roamed across what is now North America, from Alaska to the Appalachian Mountains to Mexico. These giants have played an important role in Indigenous cultures for thousands of years. Known by many names such as "tatanka," "pezhekee," and "iinii," the bison were seen as sacred and provided Indigenous ancestors with food, clothing, tools, shelter, and important medicines. Whenever a bison was killed, nothing would go to waste.

When early French explorers first laid eyes on bison grazing on the prairies, they thought they looked like oxen and called them *les boeufs*, which later translated to buffalo. As European colonizers pushed west across the United States in the 1830s, they reduced the bisons' habitat and hunted these animals for sport. Sometimes they would only take the hide or the tongue as a delicacy. Sadly, they often left the rest of this glorious animal to waste.

One infamous bison hunter was "Buffalo" Bill Cody. He was hired by U.S. Army General Philip Sheridan in 1869, who wanted to wipe out bison entirely from the Great Plains. His misguided thought was that getting rid of bison would weaken Native Americans fighting for their rightful lands. Even the future president, Theodore Roosevelt, who in 1883 traveled to Dakota Territory, hunted bison himself. However, the longer he stayed in the wild beauty of the "badlands," as they are known, the more he fell in love with the place. He admired its wildlife, especially the bison. To Roosevelt, this nearly extinct creature came to symbolize the wild American west, and he became determined to protect it.

By the late 19th century, what had once been millions of buffalo herds had lessened to fewer than 300 wild bison. In 1894, the first federal laws were enacted to protect them. Killing one became punishable by a $1,000 fine or imprisonment. In 1905, Roosevelt, who was now President of the United States, established the American Bison Society to find the remaining bison, and reintroduce them to protected areas. This included the newly established National Parks and other public lands.

Sadly, under Roosevelt's presidency, many Indigenous groups suffered as they were forcibly removed from their lands to create the National Parks that would protect the bison and other wildlife. This park, named after the president, stands as a reminder of this complex history. Broken into three parts in western North Dakota, connected by the Little Missouri River, the park is on land that was home to the Mandan, Hidatsa, and Arikara Nations. Descendants of the original inhabitants now live on the Fort Berthold Indian Reservation, northeast of the park.

In 1956, Theodore Roosevelt National Park welcomed 29 bison from Fort Niobrara National Wildlife Refuge in Nebraska. Once again, they were able to freely roam throughout the park's 46,000 acres. By 1962 the herd had increased to 145 animals.

Today, the park's total herd size ranges from 300 to 700 bison. Visitors can spot these incredible creatures along park roads, grazing near the cool cottonwoods along the Little Missouri River. While they may appear docile, park rules advise people to stay at least 25 yards away. These resilient beasts are living symbols of the wild frontier. They show the park's commitment to protecting nature's wonders for generations to come.

The Voyage Home

Channel Islands National Park, California

In the sun-soaked Pacific, off the vibrant shores of southern California, lie a cluster of five incredible islands. Channel Islands National Park, as they're known, were each formed by fiery volcanoes more than 14 million years ago.

These islands are not just any islands, they are home to many plant and animal species found nowhere else on Earth. Here a collection of nature's wonders, where creatures like the island fox, one of the tiniest canid species in the world, live only on these secluded shores.

But to reach these enchanted islands, you must cross the Santa Barbara Channel. This is no ordinary stretch of water! It is a bustling marine paradise, full of life. Over 1,000 different species call it home, from the tiniest plankton to the majestic blue whales. These waters are where giant kelp forests sway like underwater jungles, providing shelter and food to a colorful array of fish, from bright orange garibaldi to giant sea bass.

Long, long ago, these islands were home to the Chumash people who are masterful ocean navigators and skilled fishermen. Chumash ancestors passed their histories down through the generations, and one such story tells of how their people came to be. It goes like this: *Hutash*, the Earth Mother, created them from a magical plant on what we now call Santa Cruz Island, once known as *Limuw*. The people thrived, living in harmony with the islands.

However, the Chumash way of life was forever changed in the early 1800s when newcomers arrived—European explorers, missionaries, and settlers. Unfortunately, they brought diseases like measles, which took a devasting toll on the Chumash people. Many were forced to leave their beloved island homes and relocate to the mainland, where they were enslaved as blacksmiths, ranchers, cooks, and helpers.

Throughout centuries of hardship the Chumash have survived. The spirit of their island home and the memory of their remarkable boats, called *tomols*, never faded. These vessels, combining the features of canoes and kayaks, were crafted from redwood logs washed ashore after great storms. Skilled artisans and tribal members would handcraft them, splitting the logs into boards, sanding them with shark skin, and joining them together with a tar made from pine sap. *Tomols*, though beautiful, were not easy to paddle–they were heavy and challenging to navigate.

In more recent times, the mainland Chumash have come together to build boats, continuing this 7,000-year-long tradition. In 2001, aboard a *tomol* named "Elye'wun," which translates to "swordfish" in the Chumash language, a brave group embarked on a remarkable journey. They rose before dawn, setting off in the dark. They paddled across the waters from the mainland back to their beloved *Limuw*. This was no ordinary voyage; it was a daring expedition to navigate the powerful currents, fierce waves, and gusty winds. After 11 hours, they triumphantly reached *Limuw*, making a historic moment–the first Chumash-powered return to their island homeland in 150 years. It was an adventure like no other and a testament to the enduring spirit of the Chumash people and their profound connection to the ocean.

Legend of the Hoodoos

Bryce Canyon National Park, Utah

In the high desert of southern Utah lie strange and wonderful rocks, known as hoodoos. These pink-red spires stand tall and proud in Bryce Canyon National Park. Badgers scurry, woodpeckers roost, and Utah prairie dogs build their burrows in this otherworldly, rocky place. The Paiute people, who have long had a connection to these lands, believe the rocks are what's left of the To-when-an-ung-wa or Legend people.

The story goes that the Legend people trod greedily upon the arid land. They gulped the stream waters and devoured all the pine nuts from the pinyon pine trees, without a thought for the other creatures who shared these lands. A powerful god, Coyote, took notice and decided to punish them. The Legend people were invited to a grand banquet. They came dressed in their finest and most colorful clothes and settled around Coyote's great big banquet table. But before they could pick up a bite to eat, Coyote cast a spell and turned them to stone. And so they stand to this very day, stuck like rocks.

The hoodoos may have eroded over time but they're still standing tall—a reminder of the Legend people and a warning to resist greed. Although, the Paiute people never lived permanently in Bryce Canyon, they would pass through, sharing the tale of the Legend people through generations. Carefully, they harvested plants and animals for survival, always asking permission from the spirits as they took. Today, the Paiute people remember the lessons of their ancestors and continue to live harmoniously with the land.

Meet an Upside Down Flying Acrobat

National Park of American Samoa, American Samoa

Bats, those mysterious creatures of the night, are often misunderstood and associated with stories of scary, blood-sucking vampires. However, the truth is far more fascinating. Bats are the only mammals that can take to the skies, and they are quite extraordinary.

Some of them can zip through the night at speeds of 100 miles per hour. They've also unlocked the secret to a long life, with some bats living for 40 years! One of the most interesting bats of all lives in the lush, tropical rainforest of the National Park of American Samoa. It's the only U.S. National Park south of the equator and is a hidden gem in the vast Pacific Ocean. This park helps protect the rich rainforests, sandy beaches and vibrant coral colonies of four remote volcanic islands—Tutuila, Ta'u, Ofu, and Olosega.

These islands are home to the pe'a vao, or Samoan fruit bat. Unlike their nocturnal relatives, these endangered creatures are a bit of an anomaly. They fly during the day as well as the night, and with wings stretching up to three feet, they have an impressive presence. Their faces, with long snouts and pointy ears, have earned them their other name—"flying foxes."

These giant bats are very important to the islands. They play a crucial role in the ecosystem by pollinating plants, munching on fruits and helping to spread seeds far and wide. And it is thanks to them that this park was even created … in 1984, conservationists put forward a bill to protect the bats' habitat, and a few years later the park was established. To honor these brilliant bats, the U.S. government even minted a special quarter in 2020, featuring a mother bat hanging from a tree with her adorable little ones. It's a tribute to these remarkable creatures and their vital part in the beauty of the islands.

Escape to the Floodplain Forest

Congaree National Park, South Carolina

Hidden away in South Carolina, a mysterious gem awaits discovery . . . a floodplain forest. This natural wonderland thrives when nearby rivers burst their banks. The surging water spreads nutrients across the flood plain, nurturing all kinds of life. Some 400 years ago, the southeastern part of the country was once a vast expanse of 52 million acres of floodplain forests—an area about the size of the state of Kansas. But time has a way of reshaping the world. Today, only a tiny fragment of these ancient floodplain forests remains, carefully preserved within Congaree National Park.

The floodplain forest within Congaree National Park is truly special. Magnificent groves of towering trees like the bald cypress and water tupelo hang with Spanish moss. Bald eagles and wood storks soar above, while swamp-loving creatures like alligators glide through the tranquil waterways.

You might wonder how this challenging place could ever be home to humans, and that's where the marvel of history unfolds. Humans have lived amidst these forests for 10,000 years. At first, there were nomads, passing through the wilderness to hunt and gather what they needed. With time, they became skilled farmers, learning how to irrigate the land and grow crops like corn, beans, and squash. This allowed them to create permanent settlements.

However, in the mid 1500s, the people who are now known as the Congaree, faced a tragic fate. Disease, brought by Spanish explorers decimated their numbers. In the mid 1700s, many more Congaree were killed by conflicts and more disease when European colonizers claimed the fertile landscape as their own. These settlers tamed the rivers by building dikes to control the flooding and cut down trees to build vast plantations. Crops like rice and indigo were cultivated by enslaved people.

Some enslaved people found the floodplain forest to be a refuge from their cruel enslavers. Mostly men, but sometimes women and children, escaped into these lush woods, forming small communities in the forest where they survived by hunting and fishing. When supplies ran low, they would venture to nearby towns to trade with the few free Black people they could find, sometimes resorting to robbing white travelers, or even returning to the plantations to take back what had been stolen from them. Life was incredibly tough, made even harder by the relentless pursuit of their former enslavers. In fact, in 1733 the state of South Carolina offered a reward of 20 British Pounds, equivalent to a small fortune back then, to anyone who captured one of these escapees, known as Maroons.

Yet, the spirit of the Maroons stayed strong. They were resourceful and hardworking, gathering along the riverbanks, worshiping, singing, and celebrating their hard-won freedom. These Maroon communities endured through the Civil War, right up until President Abraham Lincoln issued the Emancipation Proclamation on January 1st, 1863. His declaration ordered the immediate freedom of all enslaved people living in territories controlled by the Confederate States of America. This meant that the Maroons were now technically free, though they still faced many challenges.

The Best Man in the Party: Juliet Brier

Death Valley National Park, California and Nevada

In a place known as Death Valley, a remarkable national park thrives. This park is the lowest, driest, and hottest one in the country. In 1913, the heat reached a new peak and the highest temperature on Earth was recorded—a sweltering 134° F. Today, people visit during the super-hot summer to take pictures next to the digital thermometer in front of the Visitor's Center. It often shows temperatures as high as 120° F.

Despite the intense heat, this place is still filled with wildlife. Jackrabbits use their big ears to keep cool, desert tortoises snooze in underground burrows, and bighorn sheep scamper on the mountainside. Humans too, have a rich history here. The Timbisha Shoshone people have lived in this area for centuries. They live a more modern lifestyle today, but their ancestors built brush huts that let in the breeze but kept the hot sun away. The men hunted jackrabbits and bighorn sheep, while the women wove baskets so tightly coiled they could even hold water. When the temperature got too hot, they'd retreat to the cool mountains. To the Timbisha Shoshone people, this desert was their home. They had mastered a way of life here, and it was not they who named the place Death Valley. The story behind this dark name came later . . .

In 1849, a group of migrants passed through. They were traveling to California, searching for gold, during the famous gold rush. Sadly, one of them lost their life here, and the place was named Death Valley. More and more groups made the same journey that year, and people came to call these migrants the "49ers" after the year they traveled.

One such intrepid individual was Juliet Brier, who embarked on the forbidding journey through Death Valley. She was only five feet tall and 90 pounds. She came all the way from Vermont, and had married a Methodist minister named James W. Brier. And together, they had three young sons. Their destination: California, where James wanted to go and spread the Methodist faith among the gold miners. With their wagon packed, they joined a caravan of fellow travelers, all on the same westward path.

Everything was going well, until they reached the present-day town of Enterprise, Utah. There, James decided to join a group of 49ers known as the Jayhawkers to take a short cut to California. But it turned out to be a treacherous path. Some folks gave up, and went back, but Juliet, James, and their family pressed on.

As James fell ill, Juliet had to take care of the children, cook food, make fires, and lug heavy loads on and off the oxen. At one point, their food became so scarce that they had to sacrifice some of the weakest animals, cooking them over a fire fueled by the wood from their wagons. They dried the remaining meat and, with Juliet often carrying the children on her back, trekked more than 100 miles by foot. Four of the Jayhawkers ultimately died. However, everyone in the Brier family survived, making it through Death Valley, and eventually reaching California. The Briers had three more daughters and Juliet outlived her husband, reaching the remarkable age of 99 years old. Her legendary resilience left a lasting mark on her fellow-49ers, who described her as "The best man in the party."

The Jewels of the Rainforest

Haleakalā National Park, Hawai'i

In the middle of the sparkling blue ocean, there's a magical Hawaiian island named Maui. It's a beautiful land with cascading waterfalls that tumble down from vast heights, beaches made of golden sands, and a colorful tapestry of flowers and birds. Among these birds is the honeycreeper, a small, sweet-voiced songbird. Long ago, the Hawaiian Islands were home to more than 50 species of honeycreepers. But only 17 species have survived, and one of them, the Kiwikiu honeycreeper, is in grave danger. There are only about 150 of these precious birds left in the entire world.

So where have all the Kiwikiu honeycreepers disappeared to? They've sought refuge in a small 11-square-mile haven, nestled high up in the cool mountains of Haleakalā National Park. Here, in the native forests, they flit about, singing cheery songs that sound like "chewy-chewy-chewy, chewy-chewy-chewy." These little creatures wear olive-green and yellow feathers, with a dark eye stripe that looks almost like a mask. They are also known as the Maui Parrotbill because of their beak that can slice fruit, pry open bark, and even split dead wood. To some they are the "jewels of the rainforest" because they are so beautiful and precious.

Finding a Kiwikiu has always been like searching for hidden treasure. At one point in the early 1900s, people believed they had vanished until they were found again in the 1950s. These birds were so elusive that their original Hawaiian name was lost, only to be renamed Kiwikiu in 2010, with "kiwi" for their curved beak and "kiu" for their secretive behavior.

But this bird's happy revival is under threat, and there's one deadly predator to blame—the invasive southern house mosquito. This tiny bloodsucker carries a disease called avian malaria, and even a single bite can be fatal for a Kiwikiu. These mosquitos used to avoid the high, cool altitudes, where the birds lived, but as the world's climate warms, they've crept farther up the mountains, invading the Kiwikiu's habitat. If these mosquitos continue to bite and infect the Kiwikiu at this rate, the bird might become extinct by the year 2027.

This heartbreaking news weighs heavily on the wildlife biologists in Haleakalā National Park. They've dedicated years to protecting this fragile and beautiful little bird. Instead of giving up hope, the park, along with other government organizations, has crafted a plan. First, they aim to move some of the remaining birds to distant mainland zoos where they can live and breed safely, far away from the deadly mosquito. The second part is far more complex, but it boils down to one thing: reducing the numbers of the southern house mosquito.

Scientists have a clever tool in mind called the "Incompatible Insect Technique." This involves breeding male mosquitos that can't produce offspring with wild females. If enough of these incompatible male mosquitos mate with wild females, the mosquito population on Maui would be greatly reduced.

While this may be our best hope to save the Kiwikiu, not everyone agrees because it interferes with nature's ways. Before taking such a drastic step, scientists will carefully study how it might affect the environment. Time is running out, though, and without action, this beautiful symbol of Maui may vanish forever. It's a race against time to protect the Kiwikiu and keep its sweet songs echoing through the lush forests of Haleakalā National Park.

Life on Mars

Lassen Volcanic National Park, California

Lassen Volcanic National Park is a curious, wild place. Dotted with bubbling springs and lumps of lava, this wilderness could be mistaken for an alien world, but it's much closer to home, in Northern California. In the heart of this park, there's a volcano known as Lassen Peak, reaching 10,457 feet into the sky. In May 1915, this mountain volcano woke up, and rumbled with a great eruption. It sent rivers of melted snow and rocks down its slopes, turning the forests into ashes and painting the sky gray for miles and miles.

For centuries, Mount Lassen, has been a sacred place for the Atsugewi, Yana, Yahi, and Maidu peoples. They used to hunt deer, fish for salmon, and gather acorns here in the summertime. The ancient Maidu even had a special name for the volcano, Kohm Yah-mah-nee which means "Snow Mountain," because it is always covered in a fluffy blanket of snow. The deepest snowpack ever recorded here was 27.6 feet in 1983, enough to bury a two-story building!

The whole park has been formed from volcanic activity. There are red-and-black pumice fields of the Painted Dunes, a rock avalanche known as Chaos Jumbles, and even a bubbling hot spring at Boiling Springs Lake—where the scorching 125° F water ripples and steams.

But here's where the story of this park takes an exciting turn . . . today the park is like a secret laboratory for NASA scientists. The volcanic activity in the park is very similar to past volcanic eruptions on Mars. Scientists come to explore the mysterious thermal wonders and tiny creatures living

in the heat. These creatures are microscopic organisms called thermophiles, which mean they love the warmth. Here, scientists dream of a time when they can journey to Mars and find out if similar little life forms might dwell there. NASA also invites lucky students from the nearby Red Bluff high school to join their research. These young scientists-in-training work alongside the NASA experts to help discover the secrets of the park.

Together, the scientists and students study something called astrobiology, which is all about where life comes from, how it grows, and where it might exist in the universe. They are explorers of the great unknown. In the fall, the team of scientists, a National Park Service interpreter, the students and their teacher embark on a grand overnight camping adventure to collect samples from the special springs of Warner Valley, in the southeast corner of the park. They use special tools like syringes to gather water samples and giant tweezers to catch tiny creatures. They measure the temperature, pH, and other environmental properties of the springs.

Back in the classroom, they perform lab experiments on these samples, trying to unlock the secrets of how different types of springs—hot, cold, acidic, neutral, or alkaline—are formed and how different creatures can adapt

to the sometimes hostile conditions that exist in them. Then in spring, the students return to the park, snowshoeing into Sulphur Works, a place filled with steam called a hydrothermal area. At this steamy site they once more help collect chemical samples and environmental data that the scientists will analyze.

The students' observations have helped NASA scientists better understand how life may have evolved on Earth and to further pinpoint where to look for life on Mars. Some of the students have even gone on to pursue astrobiology-related majors in college and even work for NASA!

For those who aren't lucky enough to take the class at Red Bluff High School, the park also offers "Dark Sky Days" every summer, when NASA scientists give talks about astrobiology. And there are many other adventures to be had here, such as visiting the Sulphur Works where smelly steam rises or hike on the four-mile-long (round-trip) Cinder Cone Trail. Visible from the path are the "Fantastic Lava Beds," hardened black lava flows, and farther up the trail is the black and red landscape of the Painted Dunes. This otherworldly park is one of the closest landscapes to Mars we humans can see on Earth.

A Once Booming Metropolis

Mesa Verde National Park, Colorado

Hidden and scattered throughout the rugged landscapes of Colorado and New Mexico, are the ancient remains of remarkable, long-abandoned cities, crafted thousands of years ago by the Ancestral Puebloans. These cities, unlike our bustling modern metropolises, were ingeniously nestled into the cliffsides. Many descendants of these Indigenous masterbuilders, such as the Hopi people, still call the Southwest home today.

The grandest of these cliffside cities lies within what we now know as Mesa Verde National Park, in the southern reaches of Colorado. Many rare and beautiful plant and animal species live and grow here, including wild turkeys, mountain lions, pinyon pine trees and colorful wildflowers. In the Spanish language, Mesa Verde translates to "Green Table," a name that honors the Ancestral Puebloans who farmed the tops of the mesas for nearly seven centuries! Yet, they dwelled below, carving homes into the sheltered canyon walls. They did this not out of whim, but as a clever disguise against potential enemies like the Ancestral Apache and Navajo peoples.

Today, Mesa Verde's expansive 80 square miles holds 600 cliff dwellings. Out of these, only four, namely Cliff Palace, Balcony House, Long House, and Step House, are regularly open for visitors. The largest of them all is Cliff Palace, perched at a height of 7,000 feet on a cliff's edge, protected by an overhanging rock ledge that juts out from the mesa above it. Archeologists (scientists who study human history) believe that it once housed about 100 people in 150 rooms, constructed from sandstone, mortar, and wooden beams.

The remarkable site also boasts 23 underground chambers known as "kivas", often used for celebrations and ceremonies. From above, these kivas appear as covered holes in the earth, with a wooden ladder sticking out from a small opening. At the bottom of the ladder was a fire pit near the center, alongside a smaller hole known as the "sipapu" or "place of emergence." In the Hopi people's tradition, this hole represents the point from which the Ancestral Puebloans emerged from a previous world.

To stand in the midst of Cliff Palace, one must climb 120 stone steps and four ladders! If that adventure sounds too daring, the park has more than 5,000 known archeological sites, although not all are accessible to the public. The steep 2.4-mile-long Petroglyph Point Trail leads to a rock panel with carvings that contain handprints and images of animals. According to a Hopi elder's interpretation, this panel tells the tale of two clans—the Sheep Clan and the Eagle Clan. These clans branched away from the rest of the Ancestral Puebloans and returned to their place of origin. The distinctive boxy spiral on the petroglyph represents the sipapu.

The reasons behind the Ancestral Puebloan people's departure from Mesa Verde remain veiled in mystery. Archeologists believe that it might have been drought or population growth leading to food shortages, which, in turn, compelled them to venture to what is now Arizona and New Mexico. In New Mexico, descendants of the Ancient Puebloans have established 19 Pueblos scattered across the state. One of these is Taos Pueblo, a multi-storied adobe (a building made from earth and organic materials) that has been continuously inhabited for more than 1,000 years! It's a living testament to the enduring legacy of these incredible people.

The First Hawaiians

Hawai'i Volcanoes National Park, Hawai'i

More than 1,000 years ago, a beautiful collection of islands lay untouched, surrounded by the endless expanse of the deep blue sea. Until one day when skilled adventurers sailed across the Pacific Ocean in an enormous double-hulled wooden canoe. They came from the Marquesas Islands to this new archipelago, now known as Hawai'i. These brave people were the first Hawaiians traveling to their new home.

By taking such a difficult and dangerous voyage, battling storms and enormous waves, the first Hawaiians had to be smart. They used the stars to find their way and brought much of their food with them, including pigs and chickens, and many plants, like the roots of taro and sweet potato and seeds for coconut and banana. And to ensure safe passage and survival, they worshipped natural forces like the wind and waves, and especially the goddess Pelehonuamea, or Pele, "She who shapes the sacred land."

Pele is still very important to native Hawaiians as part of their *Mo'olelo*, the history and knowledge systems that they have passed from generation to generation. Pele's story begins long before she arrived in Hawai'i. Like her people, she came from a distant land before settling in the Halema'uma'u Crater, which is at the summit of Kilauea, a volcano in Hawai'i Volcanoes National Park. Pele is a volatile goddess—both a destroyer and creator. Her fiery eruptions exploding from the volcano can wreak havoc, but the cooling lava that spills into the ocean can also form new land.

Today many Hawaiians still worship Pele and consider her part of their "ohana," or larger family. When visiting the park, which has two of the world's most active volcanoes, some ask Pele for safe travels. In 2018, Kilauea had a massive eruption, causing the summit to collapse. Today, hikers on the Crater Rim Trail can stop and see the aftermath, and feel the steam pulsing from the still active volcano—like the breath of Pele herself.

Pele isn't the only presence in the park. It is also home to the Nananana Makaki'i, also known as the Happy Face Spider because the green arachnid has markings on its back that sometimes resemble a smiling face. There are also beautiful birds like the Koa'e Kea, known as the white-tailed tropicbird, and the 'Apapane, a Hawaiian honeycreekper with a brilliant bright red body. Swimming in the Pacific, off the park's coast, are many fascinating creatures, like the Honu'ea, or Hawksbill turtle, an endangered species that can grow to weigh 150 pounds! From past to present, from ancient spirits to enchanting wildlife, a whole world awaits in this national park.

The G.O.A.T

North Cascades National Park, Washington

High up on a jagged mountainside in Washington, an expert climber navigates its way, seeming to dance from rock to rock. It's a mountain goat—and, like all mountain goats, it's such a master climber that it could be called the "G.O.A.T" (Greatest of All Time). This fluffy beast belongs to a herd that live in North Cascades National Park. Here, they roam among a breathtaking expanse of rugged peaks and pristine wilderness. The park boasts over 300 glaciers, countless alpine lakes, and more than 400 miles of hiking trails—but these goats are the stars of the show . . .

With a bearded tuft on their chin, short black horns like crowns on their forehead, and a shaggy white coat that runs down their legs, these mountain goats look as if they should belong in a meadow with friendly cows. Yet, they possess a secret skill—the ability to gracefully tiptoe on cliff-like mountainsides, out of reach of lurking bears, cougars, and wolves.

The secret to their climbing success lies in their powerful legs, adorned with hooves perfectly crafted for the tricky, steep, and slippery slopes. Each hoof has a tough outer shield, made from the protein keratin, that surrounds a soft pad. This soft inner layer allows the goat to cling to the tiniest granite rocks, while the outer hard layer allows them to grip a wider area. Sometimes, they may seem stuck, frozen in fear, mid-climb, but the hardy climbers are just taking a break.

These creatures have charmed visitors to this national park, and yet many of their secrets are still unknown. They are the least studied large mammal in North America. One mystery that has been uncovered is that they aren't truly goats at all. But rather a mischievous member of the antelope family. No matter their name, these rock-climbing champions are a true marvel of these mystical mountains!

Ancient Social Media

Petrified Forest National Park, Arizona

Off the winding I-40 Interstate in eastern Arizona is a wide-open expanse of flat-topped mesas and wind-sculpted buttes. Here a mesmerizing national park awaits—a place of 200-million-year-old trees.

These towering fossilized conifers, some of which were 200 feet tall when alive, washed into an ancient river system. Covered by mounds and mounds of sediment, including volcanic ash, these giants slumbered, hidden for hundreds of thousands of years.

Time wove its magic and the organic matter inside the logs was slowly replaced with sparkly quartz, which is a hard and heavy mineral. The clever Ancestral Puebloan people who lived here thousands of years ago (and whose ancestors still live here today) used these strong logs to build their homes. In order to preserve these singular old trees, along with the mule deer, bobcat, pronghorn, and other animals that call this special place home, Petrified Forest became a national park in 1962.

One of the most interesting artifacts in the park today is a 1,000 year-old home known as Agate House. The park sits in the middle of what's known as the painted desert, so named for mounds of rock that look almost like neopolitan ice cream, with shades of yellow, pink, and red. It has other fascinating surprises, like the archeological site "Newspaper Rock," where there are more than 650 rock carvings called petroglyphs. These were created between 650 and 2,000 years ago by the Ancestral Puebloan people who lived, farmed, or hunted along the Puerco River.

These petroglyphs are like a secret code—symbols, calendars, and markings with spiritual meanings that tell stories about the lives of the Ancestral Puebloans and their families, special events, and maybe even their favorite food. It's like an ancient version of sharing on social media, but using rocks—proof that humans have long sought to create and share with each other.

The Great Slide

Olympic National Park, Washington

Olympic National Park may be only 36 miles west of the bustling city of Seattle, but it's like stepping onto another planet. This is a sprawling, wild wonderland where gigantic trees in mossy rainforests are ready for exploration. There are steaming hot springs, and towering, mountains that call brave hikers, climbers, and skiers to their slopes. And there's lots more to explore offshore. The park stretches to Hood Canal in the east, and in the west to the Pacific Ocean. Here, the shoreline teams with tidepool life, and enormous sea stacks rise like friendly giants from the misty waters.

Archeologists have found evidence that people roamed this very peninsula for about 12,000 years. They left behind treasures—bone, shell, and stone artifacts—evidence of a thriving fishing culture from 3,800 years ago. These bygone fisherpeople hunted seals, salmon, and whales, often sailing the rough waters with canoes carved from western red cedar trees. They were the ancestors of the Makah who still live on the Olympic Peninsula today. The Makah share many stories that have passed down over generations. One such story is about a village that was buried by a mudslide 500 years ago in a mighty storm.

About 50 years ago, in 1969, another storm of great power swept through the park. It struck Cape Alava, a point that sticks out into the Pacific Ocean. As the damaged clay banks fell away, a hidden secret was revealed . . . A well-preserved ancient village emerged—the same one from the Makah story! Over a decade, archeologists uncovered longhouses, artifacts, and tools. Each finding helped build a picture of these people who had thrived here, long before the park was created. They were clever hunters and gatherers who respected the land and the sea.

Elsewhere in the park, more stories can be discovered.

At Wedding Rocks, an archaeological site south of Cape Alava, the coastline is dotted with boulders decorated with drawings of orcas and clams, the Sun and Moon, carved hundreds of years ago. High up on Hurricane Ridge spectacular views of the Olympic Mountains await. And in Hoh Rain Forest, giant spruce, cedar, bigleaf maple, and fir trees stretch and twist, covered in moss and ferns—a grand, green oasis.

Olympic National Park isn't just a park; it's a part of an ancient landscape, teeming with historical marvels and wild beauty, waiting for adventurers to uncover its magic.

The Queen of Colorado's Fourteeners

Rocky Mountain National Park, Colorado

Rocky Mountain National Park is a majestic place. The sight of the park's 124 grand snowy peaks is breathtaking. So is the height that these giants reach—77 are above 12,000 feet, and the tallest of them all is Longs Peak, which rises 14,259 feet into thin air. In 1934, Mary Cronin became one of the first women to climb this "Fourteener," as all 53 peaks higher than 14,000 feet in Colorado are called. This tough mountaineer eventually became the first woman to summit all of them.

Centuries before it was called Longs Peak, the Plains Indians who lived in its shadow named it "Nesotaieux," meaning "The Two Guides". They would climb its summit to trap eagles and use their feathers to adorn their clothing. In 1868, the famous explorer Major John Wesley Powell, became the first non-native climber to conquer its peak. And only three years later, a remarkable woman named Addie Alexander became the first non-native woman to reach the top, a great achievement in a time when few women were allowed to climb.

What Mary Cronin was later able to accomplish is a tale all the more impressive. Born in 1893 in Denver, Mary didn't dream of climbing. Girls in her era rarely hiked, let alone climbed mountains. Besides, she had to work hard because her father was ill. At 19, she became a clerk at Western Union, a company that sent telegrams. By the time Mary was 27 years old, she was so bored with her job that she started hiking with the Colorado Mountain Club for fun.

Her first hike was during a fierce blizzard in the spring of 1921, awakening her to the beauty and danger of the mountains. By the end of her first summer, she and another woman, Agnes Vaille, reached the summit of Longs Peak! By 1923 Mary and Agnes had become famous for their ability to climb just as well as the men. And they had knocked off more than 30 Fourteeners between the two of them.

In January 1925, tragedy struck when Agnes died on her way back down Longs Peak. Perhaps as a tribute to her friend or in sorrow over her death, Mary began to climb with even more passion. In 1934, she achieved the incredible— she became the first woman to reach the summit of all of Colorado's 53 Fourteeners!

To honor her, the United States Geological Survey officially renamed a mountain, previously known as Carbonate Peak, to Cronin Peak in 2005. Here in the Rocky Mountains, these magnificent peaks whisper stories of bravery and beauty into the crisp mountain air!

Charles Young and the General Sherman Tree

Sequoia & Kings Canyon National Parks, California

Sequoia & Kings Canyon National Parks are home to many giants—towering trees, deep caverns, and great mountains. A wild world thrives here. Black bears roam, digging up meadows in search of tasty roots. Southern alligator lizards dart after insects, and rare mountain yellow-legged frogs hop and leap. In the heart of this enchanting place, a trailblazer named Charles Young became the first Black National Park Superintendent. Born into enslavement on March 12, 1864, Charles's journey led him to become an example of resilience and brilliance.

Charles's enslaved parents lived in a wooden shack in Kentucky while the Civil War raged across the land from Texas to Pennsylvania. A year before Charles's birth, President Abraham Lincoln issued the Emancipation Proclamation, promising freedom for all enslaved peoples. But his declaration was dependent on which side, the southern Confederate Army or the northern Union Army, won the war.

The war raged on and on until 1865. Rather than wait and face continued enslavement, Charles's parents bravely crossed the Ohio River to Ohio, where freedom beckoned. Once in Ohio, Charles's mother, who had the opportunity to become educated, taught her son how to read and write before he went to school. Charles was a quick learner and he attended an integrated school, one of the few where Black children and white children learned together. Graduating at the top of his class at just 17, Charles was admitted to the U.S. Military Academy at West Point. This was an elite school producing the nation's top army officers. He was only the ninth Black man to ever be accepted.

West Point wasn't easy for Charles. Many of his peers and instructors believed a Black man did not belong there. They made it so tough for him that he nearly failed his freshman year. But after five long, hard years, he became the third Black man to graduate from West Point.

Charles' first assignment in the military was to command an all-Black unit in Nebraska. They earned the nickname the "Buffalo Soldiers." This name came from the Plains Indians, who believed their hair looked like the curly hair of a buffalo's coat.

Charles felt a lot of pressure in the army, knowing his success would pave the way for other Black men to succeed. He felt he must do his job better than anyone and could make no mistakes—a burden his white colleagues didn't carry. By 1903, he had earned such respect and his stellar reputation led to an extraordinary appointment—he became the first Black Superintendent to Sequoia and General Grant National Parks, which eventually expanded and became Sequoia and Kings Canyon National Parks.

When Charles arrived, the park was just 13 years old. It had been created to protect the colossal conifer trees within from poachers. Charles's mission was twofold—protect the trees and find a way to let the public enjoy them.

In the three years before Charles's arrival, the previous park leaders had only been able to build five miles of road, due to the treacherous terrain. However, during his first summer in the job, Charles and his 96-man unit of soldiers crafted a road almost 25 miles long. It stretched from the town of Three Rivers to the Giant Forest. A road so sturdy, it's still in use today. Colonel Young, as he became known, gifted the world with the awe-inspiring sight of General Sherman, the world's largest tree by volume. It reaches 275 feet tall and measures 36 feet around at its base. In 2004, a giant sequoia was named Colonel Young Tree, in tribute to Charles. Almost a decade later, in 2013, President Barack Obama established the Charles Young Buffalo Soldiers National Monument in Charles's cherished hometown of Wilberforce, Ohio.

Throughout his life, Charles lived by a saying that echoed through time: "The thing then to be desired above all others is confidence in one's self."

Where the Bears Are

Grand Teton National Park, Wyoming

Adventure awaits in Grand Teton National Park—a place of beauty and drama. The park's centerpiece is Grand Teton, a jagged peak that soars sharply 13,775 feet into the sky. Climbers, drawn by the challenge and danger, come from far and wide to claim the honor of reaching the summit. Surrounding the Teton mountain range are dense forests, babbling rivers, deep mountain lakes, and miles of wide-open grasslands.

The park may seem huge, but it's part of the even larger Greater Yellowstone Ecosystem, which stretches more than 60 miles north to Yellowstone National Park and beyond. Because there's so much room to roam, Grand Teton attracts big animals that need a lot of space, like moose, wolves, elk, bison, pronghorn, cougars, and black and grizzly bears! This is the tale of these big, burly bears . . .

Grizzlies differ from black bears in a lot of ways. Most importantly, they are larger—adult males can weigh about 800 pounds. They have a distinctive curved hump on their back, very long, curved claws, short, rounded ears, and a profile that is concave, like a dish. The biggest difference between the two bruins is in their response to being provoked—when agitated, a grizzly can become fiercely aggressive.

Grizzlies were once hunted almost to extinction by European settlers arriving in Wyoming to ranch and farm. Believing the grizzly was a dangerous nuisance, they would hunt, poison, and trap the bears. In the 1880s, there were 50,000 grizzlies roaming the continental United States. By 1975 when grizzlies were finally listed as an endangered species, there were only 1,000 left and in the Greater Yellowstone Ecosystem the population had dwindled to fewer than 150.

Being listed as an endangered species means that humans cannot hunt or kill the protected animal. As a result, the grizzly bear population has slowly recovered and today there are almost 800 that roam the Greater Yellowstone Ecosystem.

The most famous grizzly in Grand Teton National Park (and perhaps the world) is a mama bear known as "399." Born in 1996, 399 hibernates in the Pilgrim Creek area in the northern part of the park and emerges every spring near the park road with her cubs loping at her side. Scientists believe that she stays close to park roads for a reason—male grizzlies, who often kill cubs, do not like the noise and traffic on the roads. But 399 is so smart that she has learned to use this to help keep her babies safe. In 2020, at the age of 24, which is very, very old for a bear, 399 emerged with quadruplets in tow, a site that is almost as rare as spotting a unicorn. Slowly, bears like her, are helping restore Grand Teton National Park to a haven for these wonderfully wild creatures.

Rewilding the Appalachians
Shenandoah National Park, Virginia

On a map, this long, narrow, meandering national park weaves its way along the Blue Ridge Parkway—a famous mountainous road that leads to another wild wonderland: Great Smoky Mountains National Park, which stretches from North Carolina to Tennessee.

Shenandoah hasn't always been a place preserved for nature—long before the park was established, this region in the Appalachian Mountains was filled with people who lived on and farmed the land. Some families had been there for more than 250 years. Thousands of years before that, Indigenous Siouan, Algonquian, and Iroquoian communities lived here, most of which were forced to move farther west in the 1600s when white European settlers began to arrive.

By the early 1900s, as cities like Philadelphia and Washington, D.C. bustled with life, the inhabitants on the east coast craved a sanctuary to admire nature. The Blue Ridge Mountains, with their cascading waterfalls, underground caverns, misty views, wildflower-filled fields, and wooded hollows alive with deer, black bear, and songbirds seemed the perfect spot to build a national park.

To create this haven, the government had to piece together more than 3,000 plots of privately owned land, many of which were occupied by poor tenant farmers. Between 1935 and 1937, the government forcibly resettled 500 of these families, often burning their empty homes. Some joined a resettlement community near the park, while others left the region. Only 42 people were allowed to remain in their homes. Most of them were elderly residents like Annie Shenk, who had lived in the same home since 1905. Little is known about her life, but Annie was the last-remaining mountain resident to live in the park until she died at the age of 92 in 1979.

In the 1930s, when the park was established, a challenging era known as the Great Depression swept the nation. As people grappled with job loss and homelessness, President Franklin D. Roosevelt created the Civilian Conservation Corps (CCC). Unmarried, healthy men aged 18 to 25, became the center of the CCC. In exchange for six months of work, the men received uniforms, shelter, training, three meals a day, and pay.

Across the land that would soon become Shenandoah National Park, there were 12 CCC camps. Each camp was home to about 200 young men at any given time. They lived in tents that were like army barracks and ate their meals in mess halls. The work was hard, but the food was good,

and for many of the men it was their only opportunity for a job. Their mission at Shenandoah was to restore the land to its natural state by destroying manmade structures like homes, gardens, orchards, and fences and change the land into a park. Over the course of nine years the young men from the CCC built 28 sewage systems, 101 miles of trails, 136 miles of phone lines, 4,001 signs and markers, and planted 147,595 shrubs and trees! It's often easy to forget when looking at the beautiful landscape of a national park, how much human effort it takes to create one. Shenandoah would not have been possible without the hard work and skill of the young men of the CCC.

Once completed, the park quickly became a popular attraction. Today, this land of rivers and mountains is home to many plants and animals. It's open to all wildlife watchers and nature lovers. Like many national parks, the story of how Shenandoah came to be is long and winding, filled with both hardship and joy.

Return of the Wolf
Yellowstone National Park, Wyoming

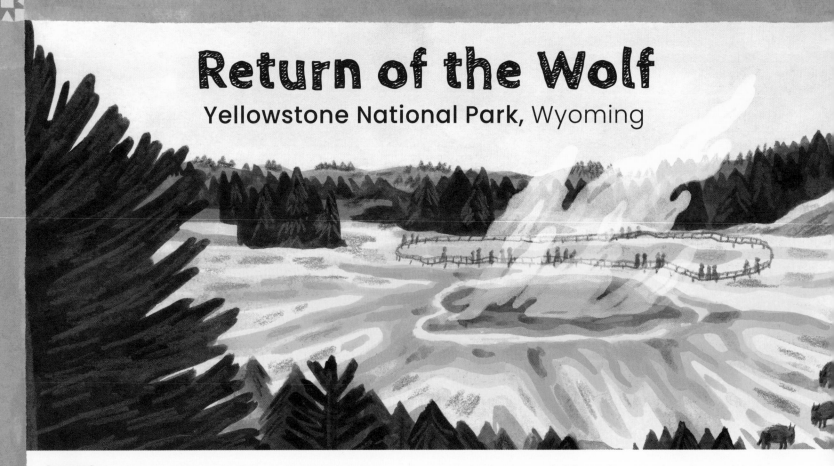

There are few national parks more majestic than Yellowstone. Established in 1872, this wild oasis, which is bigger than the states of Rhode Island and Delaware combined, was the first national park in the entire world. More than 150 years later, Yellowstone still feels like the wild west. It's a spectacular realm of rugged, snowy mountains, rushing rivers that carve through deep canyons, and an enormous lake that contains fish like cutthroat trout. There are also explosive hydrothermal features. The most famous geyser of all, Old Faithful, erupts around 20 times per day and can shoot boiling water as high as 184 feet into the air! The landscape is not all that makes Yellwstone unique. It's also home to gray wolves.

There's no doubt wolves are powerful predators. They can run up to 45 miles per hour and travel as far as 30 miles per day. Most wolves live in a "pack," a family unit that contains a mating pair and their offspring. At the head of the pack is the "alpha," normally a parent. To communicate, wolves use a haunting howl. Using their pack skills to hunt, they live at the top of the food chain, killing big animals like bison, elk, pronghorn sheep, white-tailed deer, or domesticated livestock if other food is unavailable.

Wolves may be fierce hunters, but they rarely harm humans. In fact, they try to avoid us whenever possible. But humans have still done their best to try to destroy these majestic beasts. There's no better place to understand the decline and recovery of wolves than in Yellowstone National Park. Because the wolves were such successful predators, officials decided to rid the park and its surroundings entirely of the animals, allowing them to be hunted to near extinction. By the 1940s the wolves were almost gone! When they disappeared, so did the food for many other animals like bald eagles, ravens, coyotes, and even grizzly bears, all of which would scavenge leftovers the wolf pack had left behind.

By 1974 there were so few gray wolves remaining in the United States, that they were listed as an endangered species. If the wolf population continued to decline, the animal would be lost forever. Eventually, officials at Yellowstone National Park realized their mistake. In the 1990s, biologists brought 41 new wolves from Canada and northwestern Montana to the park. This new Yellowstone pack started to grow and thrive. Today, the gray wolf population in the Greater Yellowstone Ecosystem is 500 animals strong.

For more than 25 years park rangers and field staff have kept close track of these wolves' health and their whereabouts by using small planes to monitor the packs from above and by collaring individual animals with GPS and radio monitors. Keeping the wolf population healthy is essential to preserving native plant and animal species and maintaining ecological balance throughout the entire park. Visitors might be lucky enough to watch these graceful animals race together across the landscape or, at night, hear them howling ten strong at a brilliant full moon.

Free at Last

Cuyahoga Valley National Park, Ohio

Ohio's only national park is like a long, skinny green ribbon. It runs along the banks of the Cuyahoga River between the bustling cities of Cleveland and Akron. The park is a peaceful escape for nearby city-dwellers. It is full of thousands of acres of rolling forests and farms, plus it has lots of trails for hiking, cycling, and horseback riding.

But this park isn't just about nature; it's also a place that has a fascinating story. Back in 1832, there was a long waterway called the Ohio & Erie Canal. The 308-mile-long canal ran all the way from Cleveland by Lake Erie to Portsmouth on the Ohio River. Along the canal there were boomtowns, which were lively places with mills, taverns, and stores selling all kinds of fine spices and goods from Europe.

There's just one written account, but many people believe that this canal was part of the underground railroad. The secret network that helped enslaved people find their way to freedom in Canada. In a book written in 1845, a formerly enslaved man named Lewis Clarke tells a story of his harrowing journey of escape using the Ohio & Erie Canal.

Lewis was born in Kentucky in 1815. He was the son of a white father and an enslaved biracial mother, and he had nine siblings. But when he was just seven, he was sold to another family who treated him very badly. Once, they beat him so terribly that he felt more "dead than alive."

When Lewis learned that he was going to be sold yet again, this time farther south in Louisiana, where escaping would be even harder, Lewis ran way. He crossed the Ohio River to the town of Aberdeen and eventually made his way to Portsmouth, where the Ohio & Erie Canal started. He bought a boat ticket using the name Archibald Campbell and traveled all the way up the canal to Cleveland. After waiting for several days, he found passage across Lake Erie to Canada, where he finally became a free man.

Lewis wrote, "When I stepped ashore here, I said, sure enough, I AM FREE. Good heaven!" he wrote. "... Not till then did I dare to cherish for a moment the feeling that one of the limbs of my body was my own."

Lewis then came back to Ohio after learning that his brother Milton had also escaped and the brothers reunited. But Lewis's story of bravery doesn't stop there. His youngest brother, Cyrus, was still enslaved in Kentucky. So, Lewis made a long, risky journey back to help Cyrus escape to freedom. They survived that journey, and Cyrus settled in Canada with his family while Lewis rejoined Milton. Together these two brothers traveled around the region recounting the terrible things they had experienced in slavery and why it should be abolished forever and leaving an unforgettable mark on history.

Where the Earth "Breathes Inside"

Wind Cave National Park, South Dakota

Most national parks are treasured for their stunning glacier-capped peaks, thundering waterfalls, or rugged ocean coastlines. But in 1903 President Theodore Roosevelt declared a little-explored, underground cave system as the country's eighth national park. Set in South Dakota, beneath the Black Hills, Wind Cave sprawls 150 miles long—an ancient labyrinth that formed over 300 million years!

To the Lakota people, whose ancestors have dwelled in these lands for thousands of years, Wind Cave is not merely a cave. It is "Oniya Oshoka," the sacred place where the Earth "breathes inside." In Lakota tradition, this is where their people emerged from the underground and began life on Earth. Passed down through generations of Lakota families, this story unfolds differently with each telling. This version is from the Cheyenne Creek community on the Pine Ridge Indian Reservation of the Oglala Lakota tribe.

In this story, when the Earth was still busy creating its creatures, there were two spirits: Iktomi, the trickster spider, and Anog-Ite, the double-faced woman. She was so named because her face had two sides: one was beautiful, the other was horrendous. Iktomi and Anog-Ite had only each other for company. Iktomi spent his time playing tricks on Anog-Ite, but in time he grew bored and

set his sights on tricking the humans dwelling in Tunkan Tipi. This was the spirit lodge, deep within Wind Cave.

The people who lived in Tunkan Tipi had been instructed by the Creator to wait there while the Earth was being made ready. Iktomi sought the help of Anog-Ite, promising her an end to his tricks. They made an agreement and Anog-Ite, sent her wolf companion Sungmanitu Tanka into the dark cave, laden with buckskin, berries, and dried meat in a plan to lure the humans to the surface.

The leader of the humans, a man named Tokahe, or "The First One" refused to go above. He believed they should listen to the Creator and stay underground. But those who had eaten the meat were so hungry for more that they followed the wolf to the surface. As they emerged into the open, they saw a giant blue sky and blooming plants. It was summer and they marveled at the beauty of the Earth's surface.

Anog-Ite welcomed them to her lodge, her shawl concealing the hideous side of her face. She promised to teach the people how to obtain the beautiful clothing and delicious meat they had tasted. But the work was very difficult, and the people grew tired. And, as summer turned to winter, they lacked clothes and food.

When they asked Anog-Ite for more help, she revealed the horrible side of her face and laughed at their plight. The wolf chased them back toward the cave. But it had been covered and they were trapped on the surface by Iktomi and Anog-Ite!

As despair settled over the people, the Creator, hearing their cries, discovered that they were on the surface. Furious, he transformed them into wild beasts—the first bison herd.

Time passed, and the Earth was finally ready for people to live upon it. The Creator asked Tokahe, the First One, to lead the people to the surface.

In a sacred journey, guided by prayer, they reached the cave entrance. On the surface, they saw bison hoof prints, which they followed. The bison led them to water, and from the bison, they could get food, tools, clothes, and shelter. In fact, everything they needed to survive on the Earth came from the bison.

The Creator shrank the hole of the cave to the size it is now, too small for most people to enter. But a constant reminder so the people would never forget from where they'd come.

Today, visitors can explore this special place and experience the two worlds within this park for themselves. In the dark, winding underworld, fascinating calcite blades known as "boxwork," cover the walls and ceilings in a honeycomb pattern. While in the world above ground, bison, elk, and pronghorn roam the rolling prairie, and overhead the brilliant aurora borealis pulses in pastel colors against the ink black night sky.

Whiteout!

White Sands National Park, New Mexico

There's a special place in south-central New Mexico where all around, as far as the eye can see, rolling white sand dunes stretch into the distance. This is White Sands National Park, a 275-square-mile land of shifting sand. It is home to the world's largest sand dunes.

But how did these giant sand dunes come to be in a desert so far from the ocean? The story starts in a dry lakebed called Lake Lucero where a mineral called gypsum blew in on the winds and formed brown crystals along the lakes. Over time, these crystals broke down into tiny sand grains that shifted and pressed together creating the towering dunes of White Sands.

Such a place might seem lifeless, but these sands are in fact one of the most diverse ecosystems in the Western Hemisphere. More than 220 species of birds, from the great horned owl to soaring red-tailed hawks live here. Under foot, life is thriving too, from reptiles like the pale-blue little white whiptail to the elusive nocturnal mammals like the bobcat.

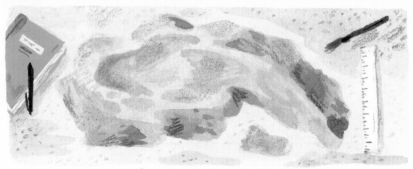
razor-clawed giant sloth footprint

Giant mammals of the Ice Age once roamed these very dunes. In 2018, paleontologists (scientists who study fossils) discovered an incredible "trackway." It had more than 100 human footprints and the prints of a razor-clawed giant sloth—a now extinct creature that stood a staggering eight feet tall!

Fast forward to today, and the dunes are alive with creatures that have cleverly adapted to the environment. Some are so well camouflaged that spotting them becomes a game of hide-and-seek. Over thousands of years, these animals, once much darker in color, have evolved to match the light-colored sands. This provides them with protection from predators like hawks and roadrunners. Some of them have fascinating names, like the Apache Pocket mouse, the bleached earless lizard, and the sand-treader camel cricket.

The first of these, the Apache pocket mouse, is an adorable nocturnal critter that scurries around the dunes at night in search of tasty seeds and insects. It uses its fur-lined pockets in its cheeks to store food and can survive for months without water. Then there's the bleached earless lizard, a tough little creature with no external ears, but a remarkable ability to hear. It braves scorching temperatures to find its way around its sandy home. Last but not least is the sand-treader camel cricket, named for its spiny legs that help it dig in the sand. This cricket comes out at night to feast on dead plants. It must be very careful because the cricket is a favorite snack of scorpions and other hungry eaters.

apache pocket mouse

bleached earless lizard

sand treader camel cricket

The fact that these animals have evolved to thrive in the unique and challenging environment of White Sands is an astonishing feat. Every dune holds a story, and every creature, big or small contributes to this mesmerizing desert landscape.

Nature's Gifts
Glacier National Park, Montana

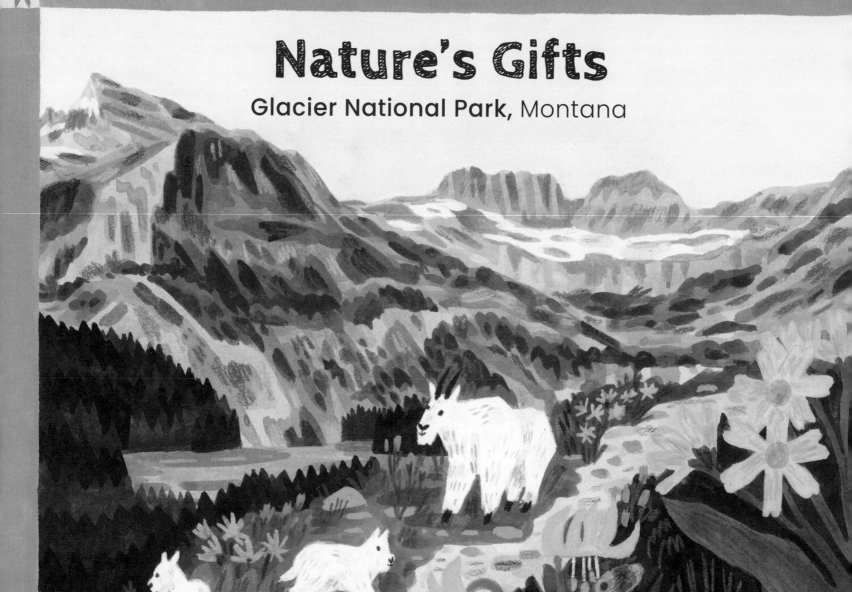

Faraway in northern Montana there is a place known as Glacier National Park. It's a part of a larger ecosystem called the "Crown of the Continent." This is one of the last wild places in North America where all the predators, like grizzly bears and mountain lions, that were here before European settlement still roam and wander.

It is a home for all kinds of animals big and small. Tiny pygmy shrews, as light as a shiny dime live here. And then, there are the elk, weighing upwards of 500 pounds!

And don't forget about the birds, fish, and all sorts of plants—they've got their own cozy spots here too.

There are also the people who have known and loved this land for thousands of years. Four Indigenous groups—the Kootenai, Salish, Pend d'Oreille, and Blackfeet—are still deeply connected with the park today. The Blackfeet, whose reservation is east of the park, have their own name for the region, "Mistakiks," which means "Backbone of the World." They believe everything here, from the land to the animals is sacred.

Many of the names of the natural features in the park come from the Blackfeet. The Belly River, for example, got its name because it's as winding as a buffalo's tummy. And Two Medicine Valley is named after two medicine lodges that were erected on either side of a creek in honor of the Blackfeet Sun Dance. One of the most amazing spots is "Ninaistako," or Chief Mountain. It's like a giant sentinel, standing 9,085 feet tall, and visible from 100 miles away. For the Blackfeet people, it is an important ceremonial and ritual site, linked to many of their creation stories. Many Blackfeet people visit the mountain to seek a vision quest, a special time to meet a guardian spirit who can share wisdom and protection.

Before Glacier National Park was created in 1910, the Blackfeet used the prairies on the eastern side of the park to find food, clothing, and shelter. They called buffalo meat "natapi waksin" or "real food." Everything else they could eat was just "kistapi waksin" or "nothing foods." But they didn't let anything go to waste—prickly nettles and thistles became medicine, food, dyes, and even clothes. One of their most important resources was lodgepole pine, which they used for building their tipis.

The Blackfeet were expert caretakers of this wild place—treating everything as a gift from nature. They shared their knowledge from one generation to the next. So, if you visit the park, try to see it through the eyes of the Blackfeet. Everything that you see, touch, and hear is special and sacred. It's a land where nature's magic dances with the stories and spirit of people who've cherished it for centuries.

Walter's Wiggles

Zion National Park, Utah

Up, up, up go the mesmerizing pink and red canyon walls of Zion National Park in southwestern Utah. A famous hiking trail zigzags up, leading daring visitors step by dizzying step on a steep, thrilling climb to the top. The adventure is worth it to see the surrounding sheer cliffs that drop to the valley floor below.

A long, long time ago—almost 12,000 years—people lived in Zion Canyon, tracking giant beasts like mammoths. The Southern Paiute, who called themselves "Nuwuvi," which means "the people," lived there for thousands of years because it was a safe, sheltered place with freshwater springs. But when pioneers came, they brought an end to the Paiute's traditional way of life, and the tribe was forced to leave its lands.

In 1872, explorer Major John Wesley Powell came to conduct a scientific survey of the region. He named the place "Mukuntuweap" in honor of the Paiute people, who called it "Moo Koon Tooh Veap," meaning "Earth Coming Up." As newcomers settled or passed through, word got around of this wild haven, and a large area was set aside to be protected. In 1919, it was established as a national park and called Zion, the name Mormon settlers used.

One of the most awe-inspiring places in the park is Angels Landing. It's a rocky spot perched at 5,784 feet, way up high above the Virgin River, which winds through the canyon. It's like being on top of the world with cliffs dropping down on both sides, and canyons in every direction. More than 100 years ago, a Methodist minister named Frederick Vining Fisher was so struck as he gazed up at it, he declared it was only fit for angels. The name stuck, and now two connecting trails allow humans to access this heavenly spot.

One particular section of trail resembles a snake slithering its way up the canyon. "Walter's Wiggles"—as it is known—is a series of 21 tight switchbacks (turns). After that, the trail turns onto Angel's Landing Trail where visitors must climb a steep sandstone cliff, with steps that were hand-chiseled right into the rock!

These trails were built a century ago, thanks to Walter Ruesch—the park's superintendent in the 1920s and after whom the "Wiggles" are named. He wasn't officially an engineer, but he loved nature so much that he wanted the trails to reflect the park's beauty. So, he made sure they were carved right out of the rock and reinforced with natural materials. These trails have stood the test of time, and they are still standing strong after all these years. This is thanks to the hard work by national park employees and local laborers who built a good portion of the trail by hand.

As well built as they are, the trails still need to be regularly maintained. In 1985, a helicopter hauled 88 cubic yards of concrete to this isolated canyon to fix part of Walters Wiggles. It took 258 flights to get all the concrete where it needed to go!

The hike might be tough, climbing up almost 1,500 feet from top to bottom. But it is a grand adventure, and the view from the top is out-of-this-world! The Virgin River flows below, and the Sun dances off the red rock walls that were sculpted by nature over thousands of years. And, once in a while, a California condor soars through the sky. This endangered species is the largest bird in North America, and it's making a comeback after facing extinction in recent years.

Zion National Park is full of cool trails, mind-blowing views, and maybe even some flying friends in the sky.

Secrets from the Depths

Crater Lake National Park, Oregon

Deep below the brilliant blue surface of Crater Lake, tunnels of ancient aquatic moss lie hidden near the lake bottom. At 1,943 feet deep, Crater Lake is the deepest lake in North America. While it's not possible to see all the way to the bottom, the water is so beautifully clear that light can penetrate to a depth of 320 feet.

Crater Lake is at the shimmering center of Crater Lake National Park in the Cascade Mountains of southern Oregon. Rising out of pine forests, the lake is ringed by craggy, often snow-covered peaks. There are two islands within: Wizard Island looks like a cone, rising 767 feet out of the water. The other island is called Phantom Ship, because it looks like a spooky ghost vessel with dark, volcanic rocky masts and sails. The park is one of the snowiest places in the United States. Each winter, snowflakes fall to the water and cloak the banks of the lake in thick white blanket. It's a fascinating place of legends and watery mysteries.

The pure, clean water in crater lake is very, very cold, almost too cold for swimming. Trails, such as the one-mile-long Cleetwood Cove trail, lead to its spectacular shoreline. And within the water, the lake's wild inhabitants swim and sway. Flashes of orange dart here and there. A strange, orange-bellied amphibian lives these depths—the Mazama Newt, a salamander-like creature that is native to Crater Lake.

How did this vast, special place come to be? A long time ago, about 8,000 years, Crater Lake was formed when a huge volcano called Mount Mazama erupted and then crumbled down onto itself. The Makalak people (ancestors of the Klamath) who lived near the volcano, believe that the mountain fell because of two warring spirits. Skell, the sky spirit, and Llao, the mountain spirit had a fierce battle. Skell won and with all his might pushed Llao deep into the mountain. The next morning, the peak was gone and in its place was a cavernous hole that was filled with brilliant blue water.

The mystery behind why the water is so clear and blue is that its only source is clean rain and snowfall. No muddy creeks or rivers run in or out of the lake. This is puzzling, because more water falls in from the sky than the amount of water that evaporates back out, but the level stays almost unchanged. Scientists are still trying to find out where all this extra water goes. Most think it might seep out through the walls of the caldera. For now, the secrets of this lake remain untold.

The Hearty Voyageurs
Voyageurs National Park, Minnesota

In a land of towering trees and shimmering lakes, there were once brave travelers known as voyageurs. The word is French for "traveler." These French-Canadian adventure seekers weren't just any travelers—they were the fur gatherers of the North. They explored the wilderness of what is now the northern United States and Canada between 1500 and 1800.

These voyageurs set forth from Montreal and Quebec City, embarking on grand journeys through the waters of the Great Lakes. In their enormous canoes, they paddled with strength, heading toward the western shore of Lake Superior. Their mission? They were hired by fur trading companies to collect animal furs to become coats and hats for the fashionable folk in faraway Europe.

But the voyageurs' tale didn't stop there. As they paddled through Lake Superior, they passed their wares to inland voyageurs, who continued the adventure in smaller canoes. Their path meandered through the heart of what we now call Voyageurs National Park in Minnesota. This is a rugged, almost entirely roadless wilderness of lakes and rivers embraced by dense forests, where deer, moose, beavers, and wolves roam freely.

Long ago, the Indigenous peoples such as the Cree, Assiniboine, and Ojibwe who lived here used the network of lakes and rivers, connected by footpaths called portages, as a vast transportation system, one as efficient and sophisticated as any Interstate highway. These Indigenous nations interacted peacefully with the voyageurs because the French-Canadians were more interested in learning to navigate the inland routes and in trading than they were in taking land. The voyageurs also relied on the wisdom and generosity of the Indigenous peoples they met, as they sought to survive the harsh northern winters.

The Ojibwe in particular had an expertise that the voyageurs depended on. They were masterful boatbuilders. They could build 25-foot-long North Canoes, called jiimaan. First, the men gathered and crafted the wooden parts of the boat—cedar for the structure and birch bark to cover it. Next, the women assembled the canoe, lashing it together with spruce root. To make the canoes watertight, they sealed the seams with a mixture of pine pitch, bear grease, and soot from the warmth of the fire. The skill of crafting these vessels has been passed down orally through the generations.

These canoes were not only practical, they were also pieces of art. A single canoe was extremely valuable and in return for one, the voyageurs traded goods from Europe such as rifles, iron tools, and cured tobacco.

The voyageurs learned many skills from the peoples they met, but they also had to be naturally tough. Their way of life was no easy feat. Before the break of dawn, they set out, paddling for up to 15 hours a day. Their canoes would slice through the water with 45 to 55 strokes per minute. Many of the men suffered broken ribs, twisted spines, or even drowned.

Yet, as a hard day came to an end, they would gather around the campfire under a starry sky. Here they shared tales, sang songs, and fell asleep under the protection of the canoes. Today, the park is named after these hearty explorers as a tribute to their incredible journeys.

The Singing Sand Dunes
Great Sand Dunes National Park and Preserve, Colorado

Colorado's Great Sand Dunes National Park is located at the eastern edge of the San Luis Valley, nestled against the jagged, snow-capped Sangre de Cristo Mountains. North America's tallest sand dunes are found here, reaching heights of up to 750 feet. This vast ocean of sand may seem lifeless, but nothing could be further from the truth! Sand-loving insects thrive here, and the surrounding grasslands, forests and wetlands are teaming with wildlife, from grasses and shrubs to elk and mountain lions.

The mystery of how sand arrived in this alpine valley that sits high and dry in the middle of the United States is a story of geology. More than 100,000 years ago, ancient lakes sprawled across the valley floor. Rivers flowing down the mountainsides added to the sediment that was accumulating in the valley. Over thousands of years, the lakes dried up and winds carried the left-behind sand toward the Sangre de Cristo Mountains. Raging storms blowing wind in the opposite direction through the mountain passes, stirred the sand upward shaping it into

ever-shifting, towering dunes.

What's strange about these dunes is that, when conditions are right, they sound like they are humming a tune. Just like humans, who can make sounds when air moves through our vibrating vocal cords, the sand makes a sound when air is pushed through its millions of tumbling grains. This mostly happens during a sand "avalanche" that unleashes in a storm or when humans hike over the dunes and push sand down the face. The sound is unmistakable, like a jet flying very low overhead

or a giant swarm of mosquitoes. For a dune to really sing, it must be at least 120 feet tall.

Because they are ever shifting, there are no designtaed hiking trails among the 30 square miles of dunes. One of the best ways to explore them and to potentially hear their humming chorus, is to hike to the top of the Star Dune, the tallest of the bunch, with a wooden sled or a sandboard. At the dune's summit, brave visitors stand on the board or sit on the sled, give a good push, then whoosh down the mountain of sand!

Welcome to Cactus Country

Saguaro National Park, Arizona

In the sunny land of Tucson, Arizona, there's a place called Saguaro National Park. It is filled with tall, brilliant green cacti known as saguaros. Some of them appear to wave with one arm, two arms, three arms, or even four! Covered in spiky thorns, these saguaros show off beautiful white flowers in spring. The oldest saguaros are like giant spiky sentinels, growing as tall as 50 feet and weighing six tons—about the same as an African elephant.

The secret to why saguaros weigh so much has a lot to do with the ingenious way these cactuses store water: The saguaro is a stem succulent, which means that it conducts photosynthesis in its fleshy column-like shape instead of in its leaves. The saguaro also has ribs that are like accordions. When the rain falls, these ribs can expand to store hundreds of gallons of water. Like most cactuses, the saguaro is very slow growing. It can take eight years to grow just one inch, up to 35 years to grow the first flower, and another 40 years for it to grow its first arm! The average age of an adult saguaro is an incredible 125 years old.

To the Tohono O'odham people, whose ancestors have lived in the Sonoran Desert for thousands of years, the saguaro cactus is treated as a living being and cared for like a friend or family member. Over the centuries, the Tohono O'odham have carefully tended and nurtured the saguaro, using its thorns, burls, and ribs to make tools and to build shelters; and harvesting its flowers, fruits, and seeds to make food, medicine, and a ceremonial wine for an annual ceremony known as Vikita. The saguaro is central to the life of the Tohono O'odham, as well as many other desert dwelling peoples. It is a special, sacred plant that should be cared for and protected.

The saguaro is important to other beings as well. More than 100 species of plants, reptiles, insects, and mammals rely on these cactuses for food and shelter. In fact, the saguaro is like Mother Nature's Hotel, a constant refuge from the scalding Sonoran Desert for a host of creatures. In early summer, the saguaro provides nectar and pollen for the Mexican Long-tongued and the Lesser Long-nosed bats. The bats in turn, pollinate the flowers. Birds like the gilded flicker and Gila woodpecker make their nests inside the cactuses' pulpy flesh, scooping out a cozy hole. And when the woodpeckers fly on, smaller birds like elf owls, screech owls, purple martins, finches, and sparrows move in. Larger birds, like Harris's and red-tailed hawks, use the saguaro for nesting and hunting platforms, constructing stick nests on the arms of the cactus. When they abandon them, ravens and great horned owls take refuge there instead. Even ground-dwelling predators like the bobcat roosts in the spiky arms of the saguaro. And when other water sources dry up, some animals like pack rats, jackrabbits, mule deer, and bighorn sheep will eat the cactuses' flesh for hydration. These plants help a whole desert ecosystem to flourish!

Back in the 1920s, the president of the University of Arizona, Homer Shantz, noticed that this precious plant was at risk because cattle were overgrazing the vulnerable Sonoran Desert. He led a movement to save the saguaro, and it resulted in the creation of Saguaro National Park. Divided into two districts, the park surrounds the sprawling city of Tucson. Saguaro West boasts low-desert views of the Tucson Mountains, while Saguaro East includes the pine-covered summits of the Rincon Mountains, which rise to a height of 8,666 feet. Both the east and west sections of the park are essential to the survival of the saguaro.

Today, the park's saguaro population is stable, but there are still two very big concerns. The growing city of Tucson and climate change threaten their home. Imagine what might happen to the Sonoran Desert ecosystem if this important, wise old being were to go extinct. It's up to humans to protect these giants and the incredible world they call home!

There's more . . .

There are sixty-three national parks in the United States, but we were only able to fit fifty between the pages of this book. The thirteen remaining parks, however, are fantastic places to explore. Here are the magical things you'll find in each one:

Black Canyon of the Gunnison, Colorado: A 48-mile-long canyon that contains 2,250-foot-high Painted Wall, the tallest vertical cliff in Colorado.

Canyonlands, Utah: A dry desert filled with fantastical red rocks and two major rivers—the Colorado and Green—that meet in the heart of the park.

Gates of the Arctic, Alaska: This vast wilderness north of the Arctic circle contains no roads, but thousands of wolves, grizzly bears, moose, and caribou.

Gateway Arch, Missouri: A 630-foot stainless steel sculpture that stands over the city of St. Louis in honor of President Thomas Jefferson.

Guadalupe Mountains, Texas: Containing four of the highest mountains in the Lonestar State, this desert park is known as "the Top of Texas."

Hot Springs, Arkansas: Nestled in the Ouachita Mountains, this park is home to naturally hot water that holds healing powers.

Indiana Dunes, Indiana: Enormous yellow-sand dunes on the shore of Lake Michigan are the star of this Midwestern park.

Joshua Tree, California: This dry desert park is named after the strange trees with spindly arms and spiky leaves that inhabit it.

Kenai Fjords, Alaska: With 38 glaciers, more than half of this park is covered in ice!

New River Gorge, West Virginia: The country's newest national park contains the deepest and longest river gorge in the Appalachian Mountains.

Kings Canyon, California: This land of towering sequoias holds the 268-foot-tall General Grant tree, which is roughly 1,650 years old.

Kobuk Valley, Alaska: North of the Arctic Circle, one of the least-visited parks in the nation has been inhabited by humans for more than 8,000 years!

Wrangell St. Elias, Alaska: The largest national park in the USA contains four mountain ranges and a glacier larger than the state of Rhode Island.

Glossary

Archipelago: A group of islands close to each other, like a family of islands in the ocean.

Archaeologists: People who study things that people in the past made, used, and have left behind.

Bioluminescence: Living things that can produce their own light, like fireflies.

Botanist: A scientist who studies the science of plants and how they grow.

Buffalo Soldiers: A nickname given to African American soldiers who served in two U.S. Army cavalry units from 1866 to 1896

Canyon: A deep, narrow valley with steep sides.

Carrion: The flesh of dead animals that some animals eat.

Crevasses: Deep cracks in glaciers, like icy canyons.

Descendants: The children, grandchildren, and great-grandchildren of people who lived a long time ago.

Ecosystem: A big family of living things and the places they live.

Equator: An imaginary line around the middle of Earth, dividing it into the Northern and Southern hemispheres.

Expedition: A big adventure or journey to explore and discover new things.

Extinct: When a species has no members left in the world.

Fauna: All the animals in a certain area.

Flora: All the plants in a certain area.

Fossils: The remains or traces of plants and animals that lived a long time ago.

Geologist: A scientist who studies Earth's rocks.

Geyser: A natural hot water fountain that sometimes shoots up from the ground.

Glacier: A giant, slow-moving pile of ice.

Habitat: The home for plants and animals.

Homestead: In the past, an area of land granted by the government to a settler for farming.

Hoodoo: Tall, skinny rock formations in nature.

Indigenous: The first people to live in a place.

Landscape Arch: A big, natural bridge made of rock.

Mangrove Forest: A special forest near the ocean with trees or shrubs that have roots in the water.

Martian: Something related to the planet Mars.

Mesa: A flat-topped mountain or hill with steep sides.

Microscopic Organisms: Tiny living things that you need a microscope to see.

Migrant: People, animals, or birds that travel from one place to another.

Naturalist: A scientist who explores and learns about plants and animals.

Petroglyphs: Ancient drawings or carvings on rocks.

Philanthropist: Someone who helps others by giving money or resources.

Pinnacles: Tall, pointy rocks or peaks in nature.

Prairie: A big, open grassy field.

Quartz: A shiny, crystal-like rock that sparkles in the sunlight.

Refuge: A safe haven or a cozy spot where animals can be safe.

Reservation: In the U.S., an area of land set aside by the government for a particular group of people, such as an Indigenous Nation or Nations, to live on.

Scavenger: An animal that eats things that are already dead.

Species: A group of living things that are similar to each other and can reproduce.

Speleologists: Adventurers who explore caves.

Stratovolcano: A big, tall volcano that can shoot out lava, ash, and rocks.

Summit: The very top of a mountain.

Superintendent: The leader or manager of a special place, like a national park.

To my mom, who fills the world with love and taught me that being outside in nature brings peace and joy.—S.P.

For my sweet nephews: W, W & A.—M.K.

50 True Tales From Our Great National Parks © 2024 Quarto Publishing plc.
Text © 2024 Stephanie Pearson. Illustrations © 2024 Madeline Kloepper.

First Published in 2024 by Wide Eyed Editions,
an imprint of The Quarto Group.
100 Cummings Center, Suite 265D, Beverly, MA 01915, USA.
T (978) 282-9590 F (978) 283-2742 **www.Quarto.com**

The right of Stephanie Pearson to be identified as the author and Madeline Kloepper to be identified as the illustrator of this work has been asserted by them in accordance with the Copyright, Designs and Patents Act, 1988 (United Kingdom).

A CIP record for this book is available from the Library of Congress.

ISBN 978-0-7112-8582-8
eISBN 978-0-7112-8583-5

The illustrations were created traditionally on paper using gouache and coloured pencils and with final touch ups done digitally in Photoshop.
Set in Julius Primary, Poppins and Cabin Sketch

Commissioning Editor: Hannah Dove
Designer: Lyli Feng
Production Controller: Dawn Cameron
Art Director: Karissa Santos
Publisher: Debbie Foy

Manufactured in Guangdong, China TT062024

9 8 7 6 5 4 3 2 1